2 00

she sparrow

a novel by ted zahrfeld

she sparrow by Ted Zahrfeld

Copyright © 2017 Ted Zahrfeld

Published by Tedz Literary Services, Fenton, Michigan

tedzahrfeld.com

Cover design and chapter icons by Jer Patryjak

ISBN-13:   978-0-9989061-0-2
ISBN-10:   0-9989061-0-7
eBook ISBN-13: 978-0-9989061-1-9
eBook ISBN-10: 0-9989061-1-5

Library of Congress: 2017907278

Printed in the United States of America   First Edition

Printed by Thomson-Shore, Dexter, MI (USA)

Dedication

To the two Sharons who love me while I reinvent myself.

To the writers in the After-Hours Writers' group, especially Erin and Ron whose support was critical.

To Char Tosi for the insights from her book, *Woman Within*.

Prologue

> I circle around God, around the primordial tower.
> I've been circling for thousands of years
> and I still don't know: am I a falcon,
> a storm, or a great song?
>
> —I, 2 Rilke's *Book of Hours*

Fear with a capital "F" overwhelms my spirit and it's not a nightmare.

Pressure rips my eyes, as I tumble to undeniable death. To slow my momentum in the darkness, I extend my arms only to discover a blur of wings—my new extensions. Wings! I am plummeting downward on wings. Instinct kicks in and I vigorously flap my limbs until my wild descent becomes a jerky flight.

Oh warrior's courage return.

Lightning illuminates two shadowy figures below.

Am not alone! Not alone.

Erratically I glide toward the men.

"Behold," points the fat one. "A sparrow. I thought the Black Blizzard eradicated those scrappy creatures."

I am a sparrow

A frail gentleman throws another shovelful of desert sand on an unmarked grave. His lined face speaks of many travels and trials, yet his eyes dance with the mischief of the desert at twilight. "We're bad actors in a white and black film." He kicks the sand and scans the dark sky as if there is a familiar presence.

"There's still an active hunt for Lilee. The Coterie say she defied their orders," responds the older man's obese brother. "It's possible they will exhume her grave, just to be certain." He smirks, "She was no assassin. What did she die for and where is her charming little dagger?"

The old man stares back, unable to answer at first, but then continues to shovel and says, "The dagger vanished like she did. Circumstances of her death have left the Corterie confounded. They stopped pursuing me."

"The Coterie, as our ruling power, has long memories."

"My Sparrow was part of my tapestry of hope against them and the pandemic. I believe she never murdered a soul. Meanwhile, to protect her we will bury the empty casket." The frail gentleman coughs slightly. "Brother, are you going to lean against that sprouting desert palm all evening? It appears the monsoons are bringing back the trees."

Mesmerized by the flashing sky, Brother finally responds, "You haven't called your daughter Lilee 'Sparrow' since the incident in the Qatar Cirque."

As a child, I recall hiding in the niches of the wall and listening to my parents. It was then father began to refer to me as his little sparrow.

Flying above the open grave I peer at my winged image reflected on the casket. My head is a mix of red-brown and gray while my body is drab with streaks down my white chest. My spirit wears an armor of lackluster feathers. I no longer appear as the warrior I sense I was once. My clanking, chattering song replaces my dagger as my only weapon.

I am my father's sparrow.

The frail one coughs again, turns, and spits a dark spot. "I'm afraid the Black Blizzard settles in my chest. There will be no singing with my blackened lungs."

"My brother, you had to settle in this godforsaken White Desert oasis, in a broken down Roman fortress. Living in the desert did not prevent you from catching the remaining effects of the Black Blizzard. Brother, return to your beloved ancient fortress you call Qasr," commands the obese one. "I'll stand watch, but the lull between the rains is a bit unsettling."

"I would ask the desert Bedouin to fill in the grave, but these superstitious people will not return soon from hiding. Even between deluges the aftermath of the Black Blizzard continues to plague them and most of the world," wheezes the frail one. "Besides, there is no one to return home to. No one to return my love," he whispers staring into the partially-filled hole. "Lilee was hungry for the affection I couldn't provide. The trouble started with that visiting British Commandant, Samman. If only I'd spent more time protecting her from his vile intentions. As a professor and gentleman farmer, I was too engrossed searching for the magical cure to prevent diseases caused by our dying atmosphere. Find me a spot to rest, Brother Jeune."

I vaguely recognize the overweight brother. Bad sensations orbit about this Jeune. But I feel warmly towards the frail one.

The obese one and frail one stumbled between rock-cut tombs settling on two broken Roman headstones. In the distance, growls of a desert cat echo among the sand bluffs and their nearby desert Roman fortress, Qasr. Through the lightning, Jeune spots a grubby sparrow hopping about the tombstones. "Look at that one motley sparrow with bright eyes, but with feathers like dull armor. I could easily crush it with my boot," he snickers. "Why are there so few of them? "

"The monsoons are reversing the effects of the Black Blizzard," sighs the frail one. "Could take decades for nature to completely restore itself."

In my brain there is a gnawing that someone or something more than the bad atmosphere is out to kill me. Quickly I fly up, hover over the head of the one called Jeune, the younger, and liberate a bodily function.

Splat. He examines his shoulder to brush off the slimy dropping. "Wretched sparrow," his eyes search the darkening skies for the culprit. "Are you resting well, Abba?"

The frail one is silent as the headstones lying around him.

My grotesque uncle calls the frail one, Abba. That is a name I called my father. I hop closer to this one called "Abba" and peer into his face. Night sky flashes expose his face. Yet I can't distinguish the color of his eyes. My Abba has two different colored eyes: the right emerald, the other indigo. I can't be sure. But it is his scent that captivates me, an earthy smell of a man toiling with frankincense saplings. He appears to be my Abba, Father, my first love. My muscular, beautiful father is a dry desert twig. Frail one, rest peacefully among the gravestones— after all the troubles I caused you.

Too late Jeune's boot strikes, tumbling me into the sand.

"What is she up to, Abba? Get out of here you pitiful, scrawny piece of bird meat."

My spirit is wounded more than my plumage as I recall a verse from Abba.

**I watch
and am like a sparrow
alone on the rooftop.**
Psalm 102:7

One

Fragments of remembrances are falling together. I, sparrow will take you back. My life, we will watch unfold as if it happens in the present moment. Let the memories begin.

 My earliest recollections are of my youth in our renovated Roman fortress on the old spice route in the Egyptian White Desert. From my second-floor watchtower bedroom a few of father's prized novels are my world.

Through the bedroom window, I watch Father helping Bedouin prune the myrrh and frankincense hybrid trees. Stripped to his waist, sweating, he glistens in the hazy afternoon heat.

As a teenager I fantasize about Abba in my secret poem:

If I were a son
teach me to play soccer tough.
If I stumble beat me. How
I long for the swoosh of the myrrh
branch. Celebrate the bruises
upon my body. Treasure
the pain as kisses.
An Arabian stallion I am
swerving, charging, over the sand dunes,
mouth foaming nostrils flaring

longing for more.
My pain is love.
Am I a foolish, foolish daughter?

Oh Father, my craving
in the night come like a thief.
For whom do I save myself?
Abba, you are my true love.
I ache for your affection
yearn for your gaze to caress.
Am I a mad, mad girl?

You are the rain; I am the ground;
 nourish me, a bud.
A butterfly, devour me
 like a desert spider.
Am I an insane child?

Think of me not as your daughter
but as a woman, a mirror
to reflect our love.
For your honor I would
give my life.
I yearn for you with my gift of self.
All I seek is your devotion.
Let me glow and burn
in the fire of your love.

Observing Father cut the dead frankincense branches, I
want to kill my idiotic desires. I drive my right thumb into
the deepest cross impression until it bleeds. These imprints
on my wall were scratched by celibate hermits who inhab-
ited our fortress in medieval times. But my ramblings will
not cease:

Longing for your embraces
a doe hungering for spring water.

I am a sparrow; you the hawk.
My heart is dedicated. Pledge
my pitiful life, servant, slave.
Father do you love me?
A thousand yeses carried on the desert wind.
If only my love were so sure.
Am I a ridiculous laughable daughter?

Whisper tenderness to your absurd child:
night into day; dark to light.
At dawn the moon magically still
shines upon me, your lotus, Lilee
Make me bloom.
With your love I am a woman.
In turn if only I could love as a wife
but I am an irrational daughter
imprisoned by my fidelity.

My affection I vow
a moth to flame.
My silly heart will never swear
Nor ever consummate its feelings.
Am I an insane girl?

From that day, I, Lilee a foolish, foolish child, secretly
imagine myself united to Father. Will I ever love another as
I do you, my Abba?

Two

That hazy afternoon outside our Roman Qasr I watch with sad sparrow eyes Father deal with her youthful emotions, aspirations, and a treasure map.

 Sitting on a stone bench in the arid courtyard, my exhausted father attempts to read a pirated copy of *John Le Carre's Tinker Tailor Soldier Spy.* While I wait to speak, I poke the cracked mud with my sandal. His clothes exude an earthy aroma of frankincense and myrrh from the trees which he pruned all morning. I drink in his smell. Sometimes I fantasize stealing his shirt to keep his scent near. A single silver lock falls across his sweaty brow and he looks up.

"Father, when you were very young," I nervously pose the question, "did you ever feel wonderful one day and then the next morning really strange?"

"What do you mean?" He straightens.

I hesitate, but the gate to my feelings is unlatched. "You know, funny. Like tingling all over."

"Are you ill?" He places a callused hand gently on my forehead.

"I'm fine." I cover his large hand with my small one, which he quickly withdraws. "It's inside," I point to my small breasts. "Warm feelings run from my toes to my head. Other times I feel blah. Neither hot nor cold."

"When do you have these emotions?" Two more silver locks cascade over his growing perspiration.

"Oh, sometimes watching the spring buds on the pomegranate trees." I hesitate, "but mainly noticing this Bedouin boy. He has a pretty face. I'm taller than him. Want to speak to him . . ."

"Does this Bedouin have a name?" Father straightens his silver locks.

"I want to ask him, but I'm afraid of these funny feelings," my sandal digs the dry mud deeper.

"These sensations are normal. Madame is better qualified to address these changes in your body. Meanwhile, I think it is best you don't have contact with the boy." Father seems relieved to sidestep my concerns. "Was there anything else bothering my little Sparrow?"

I'm disappointed with his solution because I suspect mother Madame will be of no help. "Yes. I've decided on what I want to be."

"Which choice has my Sparrow contemplated?" he smiles.

"Yes, I've definitely made up my mind."

"Girls don't decide," he laughs. "They are married to suitable young men."

I know my Abba is playing. "I will be a warrior for the Wise Men like in the stories you've told and save people. Did their caravan camp in our oasis?"

"The caravan staying in Farafra is a legend and the Magi didn't save people. They brought gifts to honor a great King."

"Then I will take bread to the poor Bedouin . . . I will be a kind and wise warrior," I beam.

"You absorb too much warrior business from the books you steal from my shelves."

"But for you, Abba, I will be a fearless warrior. If an enemy comes to your door, I would nail his head to the door lintel," I raise my voice, "and cut out his tongue and feed it to the desert cats."

"Calm yourself, Princess," he says gently. "You chatter like a poet of ancient times."

"I enjoy studying modern poets," I say, coaxing the sand flea over my sandal, "and writing some poems by myself."

"What is a poem to you?" Father asks as if he is wearing his professor's mantle.

Taking a long breath, "My words express who I am."

"But you're just a little girl with big words," he chuckles.

The laughter stings and I fight the tears, "my words reveal my feelings."

"My tiny sparrow has big emotions," he smiles and quickly asks, ". . . and your favorite poet?"

"E. E. Cummings, because he doesn't do all that rhyming."

"Perhaps someday my poetess will publish her work," then adds jokingly, "my sparrow may well accomplish more as a would-be assassin does in your novels."

"Am intrigued by these characters, but who really is an assassin?"

Father pauses unsure whether to answer truthfully. "An assassin is a paid murderer of an important person. It's usually done with stealth and under the direction of another authority. It's an old profession."

"Is an assassin admired?"

"Yes, among his peers, if he's any good."

"It's an art then," I decide.

"No, it's a dirty business, depending on who gives the orders." Looking at the dried mud he is sorry that he opened the assassin discussion.

"Who determines who dies?"

6

"That's the problem," he says thoughtfully, "some bad people may deserve to die. On the other hand when evil people make the decision, good people are executed."

"I will only work for good people."

"The assassin has two dilemmas." Abba holds up two fingers. "Finding a benevolent power to be his employer."

"The other?"

"Even though he is following orders, the assassin is the final judge," Father states seriously. "He looks the accused in his eyes and squeezes the trigger. Could you do that?"

"Yes!" I see in his eyes disappointment. But I am thrilled with the glamour of being an assassin.

"At one stage your young heart was with photojournalism. Do you remember? Then a poet and now without much thought an assassin. If I had my choice, I'd make you a poet. Poetry is less dirty and you can still kill prominent people with your words." Abba places both his hands on my shoulders.

In my head I shut out Father's words with the clicking of an old film in which I am the star of high adventure. *Perhaps a warrior assassin can publish poems of her exciting exploits.*

"As a photojournalist you could investigate the legend of the lost Magi treasure." Abba's face turns grave and ponders, *must divert her from this crazy idealism of being an assassin.*

"What is it Abba?"

At first he chooses not to answer. I practice my new warrior's patience. After some deliberations he declares, "Sweet Lilee, what I'm about to reveal is a secret I've concealed for years, only to be shared at the right moment. I think this may be that time." I see his struggles, and continue to sit in silence, realizing its importance.

"An old blood treasure map came into my possession from the Bedouin who swear it's authentic. The map

7

supposedly shows the location of the legendary lost Magi caravan of gold."

"Blood map?" I gasp.

"Many lives were lost fighting over the bloodstained skin. Many families split apart."

"Did you search? Why aren't we still looking? I'm strong. I can dig quickly."

"My Sparrow, the desert is an endless sea of sand. The Bedouin know every shoal of the Sahara. Over generations they searched. Found nothing except the excuse to kill each other. Besides the map is vague concerning where the gold is buried in the shifting desert. It would take a miracle to find the Magi gold."

"Where's the treasure map hidden?" I jump up and down.

"After years of bloody fighting the Bedouin elders decided to tell their people that the map was destroyed. Instead they demanded I, their trusted friend, conceal the map which they could not bear to demolish. I believe in the legend of the vanished gold and honored their request."

"Can I touch the map with the bloodstains?" the warrior sparrow in me chirps.

"Perhaps in the future. For now the map is buried in an unmarked clay vessel tomb among other unmarked clay pots. Its exact location is lost even to me. The jar was misplaced with the others scattered throughout our Roman Qasr." Observing my sullen face, Abba offers, "the time is right for you to learn the ways of a weapon whether you become a Queen photographer, poet laureate, or . . . err . . . Princess assassin."

Three

I, Sparrow remember her reclining at Father's feet and listening, as he spins biblical tales. Two stories he returns to often are the lost map and the deluge.

 "Once upon a dark night," he begins, "a devil of a sandstorm devours the Magi camel caravan heavy with gold, frankincense, and myrrh. The lone survivor, the legendary fourth Magi with his dagger draws a map in his own blood. To preserve the blood document he carefully secures it in his dagger's scarab which he attaches to his tortoiseshell cat. The dying Magi is swallowed by the sands with the dagger held across his chest."

Father shifts in his chair and turns, "Lilee, you might ask what happened to the lost gifts?" Before I can respond Abba continues, "Myrrh tears dry into grains of more sand. Frankincense vaporizes like a perfume of angels' wings. But a caravan of gold sufficient to establish a kingdom on earth endures for those pure of heart and brave enough to search. Tradition says Judas Iscariot found and spent the gold on wine for the poor. Another legend has the gold hiding in the Grecian monastery of St. Paul. One of the seemingly true facts," he smiles. "The name of the Magi's feline is 'Flower.' She disappeared in the desert, but through a chain of unknown events, the blood map came into the Farafra

Bedouin's possession. They doggedly continued to fight and . . ."

"Tell the deluge story," I bounce up and down.

"It's getting late; this tale will be short." Taking a deep breath, "Once a long long time ago the people of the world were very very bad. The Creator of the universe saw no hope for these people, but in his loving mercy, he would save some to start over. He instructed Noah to build an ark to save two of each species."

"Species," I ask with a puzzled look, "bugs?"

"No," he smiles, "two of every creature, man, and animal."

"Did the horned vipers share a cabin with the oxen?"

Ignoring my question he emphasizes, "The world was destroyed by a flood, a deluge. And the Creator promised never to demolish the world again with a flood. Interestingly the Bedouin believe that the world will be saved by a deluge. If there were a huge man-made or natural disaster the waters would cleanse . . ."

"I don't like the deluge story. It's terrifying." But I am safe, happy in his presence.

Will we ever search for the gold, Abba?"

"Possibly when you are older Princess."

Four

Imagine Abba, teaching her to shoot in their culture. Is he preparing her for a sinister profession out of love or fear? Then there's the blood map.

 Spending more time with Father, the blood map is soon forgotten. "Girls don't play with straw dolls." I singsong his favorite chant to me. Rounding the watch tower of our Roman Qasr, my heart leaps to see him holding the prancing Arabians, "Greek" and "Roman," his most prized possessions. He bartered with the desert Bedouins for a pair of high-spirited Arabians who were bred to what he considered physical perfection. These Arabians are of a Kehilan strain, standing fifteen hands tall and deep chested, powerful. "Greek" is a gray, and "Roman" is a chestnut.

"Why is my little Sparrow singing?" he chuckles.

Of the litany of my names, his favorite is "Sparrow." I am his pet. Seemingly he loves me as a kind of little animal. I may not have the strength of my Abba's Arabians, but as a sparrow, I am faster and have special powers.

"You know, Madame flinches when you call me Sparrow. She doesn't like that nickname." *I'm too happy to care.*

"Madame would be more infuriated if she knew what we were executing this evening in the desert," Abba sings back. "Take Greek, he's a devil today, and as I recall your favorite."

Mounting our steeds, we ride a short distance into the cooling desert, laughing and singing. "Little sparrow one, little sparrow three. Can you hide from me . . . ?"

The evening desert is a mirage of dying lights and growing shadows. Locating a shallow valley, Father sets out a dozen clay pots as targets. He found them hidden in the Qasr.

"The new culture," he shouts walking back to where I hold our Arabians "does not encourage anyone, especially women, to learn the use of a weapon."

"A gun is ugly; must I touch the metal?"

"A pistol is a beautiful weapon, Sparrow. It will be valuable in your future. If nothing else it will give you confidence in any profession. And should you evolve into a Yahweh forbid assassin, your pistol will be the tool of your trade." He shudders, "And you will learn to love it."

"Are we hiding in the desert from Mother?"

"No," laughs Father, "you're less likely to hurt the desert or shoot yourself in the foot."

"I don't want to shoot my foot," the Sparrow in me cries. "I don't want to kill anything."

"No, no. We are not going to kill," he says firmly. "Nor even hurt one of Yahweh's desert creatures, but remember an assassin does hurt its victim."

My Abba turns to God when he needs authority. In this instance, I feel he is mirroring God's love for all His creatures including me. *How can I be a dazzling assassin and not harm a soul?* The setting sun halos my Abba who appears godlike. My vow is never to offend Abba's love as I would never transgress my heavenly Abba.

"I love the Desert Jerboas' large eyes." Abba dries my tears. "The rodent's big ears flop as she scurries searching for food."

"It's all right. We will not harm the Jerboas. Let me show you the pistol we will be practicing with. It's called a Glock 27."

While he holds the gun I run my hand over the handle tracing the deep engraving of a female figure. "Who is the pretty lady?"

"She is the Statue of Liberty. The beautiful lady stands in the harbor of old New York where your father lived and taught as a young man." Abba stands tall.

"Why does she stand in the water?" I puzzle.

"The lady doesn't get her feet wet," he laughs. "Even today in this faraway land she magnificently stands for freedom and justice, welcoming the downtrodden and unwanted." His different colored eyes burn with outlandish fire into mine. "Perhaps you'll start a new breed of assassin who stands for justice and mercy."

"Does this mean I'll never be forced to kill?" I blink, unable to divert his focus.

"Killing is an assassin's way of life. I pray you don't choose this life." To change this hurtful conversation he holds up the ancient Glock. "This is an anniversary model which celebrated the hundred and twenty-fifth anniversary of the Statue of Liberty. My father gave it to me when I was a young man leaving for war." Father turns with a faraway stare to the West. "It was a birthday gift. I wore it close to my heart. My father is gone, a long time. Someday this Glock will be yours."

The Sparrow in me attempts to project into the future. *The Glock wearing the beautiful lady will give me freedom. Maybe it has magical powers.*

"The Glock holds no sorcery. You, my Sparrow, give it or any weapon its power." He brings the pistol close to his chest.

"Do you love me?" I blurt, wishing he would hold me close to his heart.

13

"Princess, I love you very much," he affirms touching me lightly on the head. "No matter what Madame or 'they' say, I will always love you," Abba declares with such great firmness that I shiver.

"Who are *they*?"

"Perhaps in the future," he instructs, "bad people will tell you terrible stories about me."

"Bad stories?"

"My life," Father whispers, "requires I bend the truth at times and even appear to do terrible things. On the surface, these actions appear evil, but they are for the good. My enemies will try to persuade you otherwise."

"Abba, you scare me." Grabbing him around the waist, I squeeze hard. "How is a grower of trees evil?"

"Nothing to concern my Sparrow now." Pulling my arms away he offers me the Glock. "Someday this weapon will be your best friend. You must practice."

Wrapping his hands round mine, he demonstrates how to hold the Glock and point it. Together, with my hands in his, we squeeze the trigger and a clay jar explodes. The sharp noise is frightening and I jump back from the impact. "*Yow*," screeches the Sparrow in me and I drop the weapon into the sand.

Retrieving the Glock he carefully wipes off the sand. "Try again. You'll become accustomed to it like your favorite book."

Abba places the Glock in my hands and encourages me again and again. Pointing at the clay pots, I squeeze the trigger three times. Puffs of sand jump from the desert, but the pots do not break. *Wish Father and I could run and chase each other, anything but hurt those clay pots.* Turning to admire father, *even a desert sparrow can flit with her mate in the warm desert sand in a dance of love.*

"Princess, Princess," Father demands, shattering my dream, "you need to try harder. It's important."

"Do you love me?

"Yes, of course, Princess. But the evening light will be leaving shortly. You must concentrate. See how I squeeze gently."

Reluctantly, I point and press the trigger twice. Nothing breaks. Again and again I shoot. Finally a clay pot shatters and bursts like a skyrocket. My heart jumps and a warm exhilaration pervades my body.

"Wonderful, my Sparrow," Abba applauds. "Soon I will call you Falcon, for you will always capture your prey."

I only want to be his Sparrow, basking in his warm glow, I am his true love.

"For all times you'll be my honored Sparrow," he announces.

I continue to aim and squash the trigger. After many attempts, I break another clay pot. The hot sensations flow over me like love. I see the joy in my Father's face. Both his emerald eye and indigo eye are on fire and I am happy. The sparrow in me learns quickly; the clay pots explode more often. When the eleventh pot disintegrates, a darkly stained roll tumbles into the sand. Father retrieves it and slowly stretches out the small skin chart.

"Is it . . . the blood map?"

Without answering directly, "Of all the pots to choose carelessly. I must destroy this vile document before . . ."

"It's the answer to your prayers. The treasure could buy many frankincense and myrrh trees," the sparrow in me cries.

"The chart is evil." Father begins to tear at the skin. "Where to bury this damn . . ."

"Wait. Hold on." I jump up and down creating sand devils. "If the map is, so the Bedouin say, destroyed, may I keep it?"

"Too dangerous, your young life would be in jeopardy."

"Who thinks that a young girl carries a treasure map?" I plead with him. "Much safer than a clay pot so easily found in the Qasr. I will always keep it with me as a souvenir of this time. The day I learned to shoot the Glock." *Yet, in truth, I will keep the map close to my heart in remembrance of you, Abba.*

Abba, always the rational professor, studies me. "All right, but always keep it hidden on your person. And for your safety don't reveal its existence to anyone, even Madame."

"Of course Abba." He hands over the tiny fragile skin, which I place in the pocket over my heart.

After shooting the last jar, "Well done, my Princess, my Sparrow," asserts Abba gathering the stallions. "You will be a worthy adversary. A falcon. A terror to your enemies in any profession."

"Sparrow, I am only your sparrow. Sparrows do not have enemies," I shout, but Father does not hear above the nervous Arabians. He could've explained that indeed oasis sparrows have many enemies.

My revelry breaks when Father fires. The Glock finds its target, a horned viper. The venomous snake wiggles once, and then lies motionless.

"There are some creatures that deserve to die," Father says calmly. "Even the evil has some good to give." He cuts off the snake's body, leaving the horned head for the beasts of the night to feast upon. Holding up the limp viper, he grins. "A tasty morsel to add to our evening meal."

The snake which I don't love maybe I could shoot, but another person? "Do you love me, Father, because I am your flesh?"

Abba does not respond, pretending to straighten the stallions' reigns. My heart ponders his detached affections.

Fighting off the black haze, the sunset throws its last bolts of golden red across the sky. "Little falcon one, little falcon three. Can you hide from me . . . ?" sings Father.

"Little sparrow two, little sparrow four," I chime back imagining my Abba's love wrapped around like wings. "Will always find you more . . ."

With all the clay vessels broken, I'm honored by his trust in me. As we amble home, wave after wave of sensuous feelings washes over me. *Is this how it feels to be in love?*

Five

Wrapped in father's affection doesn't protect her from the harsh outside world. Fondly I remember her first encounter with Commandant Samman who arrives unannounced at Farafra oasis searching for solutions.

 A Roman cemetery, a limestone chapel, and groves of lush trees are my normal playgrounds in our oasis. The few Bedouin children are wary because I blossom taller, gangly, more boyish. The Bedouins speak a strange language and play even weirder games. My attempts to join cause them to run and hide. The Bedouin prefer to chase the small flock of sparrows which calls Farafra home than to play with me. They believe that spirits inhabit the sparrows which give the birds freedom to move through the air. These spirits see into the past and possess magical powers.

At these times I am a spirit trapped in the body of a sparrow.

I hunger for the liberty which the oasis sparrows' possess. I don't need friends. Because Father doesn't have time to spare from his exotic plants and mother couldn't be bothered about my magical skills, I become a bird spirit, creating make-believe stories. Overwhelmed by the intoxicating aromas, I stretch out my arms and run among the eucalyptus, pomegranate, and citrus trees. Imagining myself a sparrow, I hide behind falling tombstones. When the Bedouin children skip by, I leap from the shadows. On their faces I see their past, the passion and the pain of the blood map. They run screaming.

I am She Sparrow.

"Lilee, why terrorize your friends?" calls Father, rounding the crumbling walls of the cemetery chapel, keeping pace with a fast-walking, lean stranger in faded camouflage.

"Forthcoming, the next phase will be implemented by a military team. Doctors will soon, very soon implant a small communication device which provides access to the InterSocial. Have your people ready, including the Bedouin," commands the stranger in a military British accent.

Flapping my arms, I sit cross-legged and listen.

"My little sparrow needs to restrain her imagination," says Father, smiling at the stranger. "Captain Sam from the Nile River region will be with us a short time. Take him under your wing and show him Farafra."

"*Samman*, provincial Commandant Samman," the stranger corrects with a strong accent.

"So sorry," laughs Father imitating his accent, "we're a bit abso-bloody-lutely informal in the desert."

"Apologies acknowledged," says the stranger with tight lips.

"Did you bring me a present?" Catlike, I stare at the stranger.

He glares back without answering.

"After our visit to the Nile River," I turn towards Father. "You promised a pet crocodile."

"No, we might very well become the dinner of Mister Crocodile," Father says.

19

"Egyptians were the first to tame felines," interjects the stranger.

"Father, yes. That's what I want—a tortoiseshell-colored tabby," I plea.

"Cats are mysterious, never owned by people," instructs Father, "they only tolerate us."

"I have magical powers," I say, waving my arms. "I can tame cats and fly like a sparrow."

"Samman, I leave this situation in your good hands," Father then says over his shoulder to me as he retreats home. "Show the Commandant around, but not all 100 of our Qasr's rooms. One could become lost for months in one of the windowless rooms."

"Do you truly imagine yourself a starling?" asks Samman in his crisp accent.

"Sparrow. Sparrow, sparrow," I yell as I race around a eucalyptus tree; I feel my feet beginning to leave the ground.

"You're quite a young lady." He leans against a dilapidated gravestone.

"Not a lady, but a loveable sparrow with bright eyes and feathers the color of dappled dewdrops. And I've magical powers."

"Bloody well you have," pointing to a grove of trees beyond the cemetery being pruned by a group of Bedouin. "What does your father cultivate?"

"An impresario. He grows myrrh for its oils and the frankincense to whiff." Standing toe to toe I look into his narrow brooding eyes, "With my miraculous power I'm able to read minds."

Samman backs away, "I wouldn't think there's much of a bloody crop market in the desert."

"Since ancient times, myrrh is used as embalming oil." I think back to all the knowledge Father lovingly fed me. It excites me to share it with Samman. "It symbolizes death and all the suffering that goes with it."

"Must be arduous to farm exotics."

"Myrrh is a thorny bush, very temperamental. Frankincense is sturdy and reliable as religion. The sap is harvested like tears and I think called Sacra or sacred."

"Cultivating outlandish specimens in this forsaken land is a grand shambolic waste," he pans the small orchards with his hands.

"Bedouin and Father combine the best of myrrh and frankincense."

"Bedouin are a miserable lot. No discipline."

Ignoring his criticism, I continue to explain, "The one is nurtured with the more sturdy stock to accept the other, not as a parasite but like an orchid," amazingly, Father's tutelage spills forth, "to grow upon the shoulders of the host plant yet not sap the strength of its benefactor. The hybrid produces an oil which, in fact, can be used for both embalming and the sweetest of perfumes." Without thinking, I move closer to breathe in his sweet scent.

His eyes narrow, "Your entrepreneurial father is in the funeral business?"

Stepping up on a low grave marker I look down at Samman. "Rumor has it that using this newfangled fluid, a body remains unspoiled for centuries. Works like a form of mummification without the wrappings." Spontaneously I leap at Samman. Startled he manages to catch me, and for a brief second, I take another opportunity to inhale his syrupy scent. "The sappy tears of Father's pet trees create the most bizarre fragrances."

Pushing me back abruptly, he says, "The ancient French nobility would have died for a mere essence of such perfume. And the remunerations to be preserved 100 years would be enormous."

Laughing to the point of crying, "If the three Magi possessed such a wonderful concoction, they would have brought only two gifts."

"The wise men are a fairytale for children."

"The God of Jacob. His Son was born in a stable," I poke my finger into his dusty camouflage shirt, "and He had many visitors including the Kings of the East."

"More propaganda," pushing my finger away, "the majestic son of God would have chosen a palace."

"Love, he did it out of love, Sam." I blush at using his shortened name. "He didn't need a Cairo Ritz-Carlton."

Turning red, Samman changes his inquiry, "There are reports that secret antidotes are being developed in Farafra concerning the Black Blizzard."

I eye him critically. "Beware, I can read your thoughts."

He takes no heed and continues on. "Truck caravans must take a blooming century to bring agricultural supplies." Samman thinks, *based on Jeune's intelligence her father is supposedly developing an antidote for the effect of the pandemic and now a marvelous perfume. The antidote is bad news for our business yet the perfume could be profitable. I must confirm the details before I can report back to the Coterie. This Lilee sparrow girl is wonky.*

"Father uses his nonliving pet—the old Twin Beech to fly everything in. He barters for our necessities since our Credits are scarce."

"Affirmative," says Samman, "that old Bush cargo plane from the 1970s with two Pratt and Whitney nine cylinder engines and an H-tail, parked behind your Qasr." He states to impress me. "That's his non-pet?"

"Abba does have his pets—Arabian stallions. Sometimes I think I am his pet. But then he wants to make me into a son."

"In this culture, a son is the true heir," puffing his muscular chest, "a male would discover the blooming means to accumulate vast amount of Credits."

"Around their campfires Bedouin brag of a map leading to much gold buried by a Magi," I say casually. "Gold is better than your old Credits."

Samman's face turns from surprise to serious curiosity. "Have you heard of such a fine treasure map? And the narrative of a fourth Magi?"

"Bedouin whisper many tall tales."

"And what is it that they say?"

"Thought you weren't interested in fairy tales. The stories are old, I don't remember them." In an effort to divert what feels like an interrogation I say, "Abba brags that he cruises at 200 miles per hour." Covering my ears, "I block the engines' high-pitched scream which could awaken buried treasure."

"You call him Abba?" he screams.

"He is my loving father," pointing heavenward, "just like my other. Sometimes, I yearn for both my Abbas like my Arabian stallion 'Greek' aches for a desert spring."

"You know what I'm bloody yearning for?" Smiling for the first time, he chases me about the cemetery until Father's supper bell causes me to run home squealing.

Six

Most every day she rendezvouses with Sam. These memories hurt because of what he did to her. Rather relive the pungent smells of a family meal in her great dining hall.

 At one end of an enormous table is Abba haloed in white by the morning light. Opposite is Madame, not so blissful. "Whom are you keeping company with," shouts Madame. "You know you will be promised."

"I offered to help Commandant Samman understand our oasis. We only talked about the farm."

"Where and how many times did you and Mister Samman have these clandestine encounters?" she raises her voice.

"Among the date palms, a few times."

"When are you planning to run away with this handsome Captain?"

"Talking. We only speak about Father's Arabian steeds and the Magi and the farm." Standing tall, I push my hands into the table until they turn white, ". . . and he's a Commandant. Samman reveals mysterious far off lands and dreams of bringing the InterSocial to Farafra," and I think, *Sam makes my heart leap a little, but not like Abba does.*

"He's only a paltry officer, Lilee, you are evil," Mother porcelain white complexion seems to crack. "You are not the obedient daughter I demand."

"Samman questioned me about the Magi gold lost in the White Desert." I weakly offer him to her as another victim, like myself.

"Secrets of the wise men's gold are to be kept hidden in our desert," she gestures sweeping the air, "among the bones of caravans and Romans."

"I didn't share all I knew of the treasure map. I avoided his questions, only telling him that it was lost, and had been for many years. That's all Madame." I smile inwardly with joy that when Sam reached for my hands, I didn't pull away.

Mother scowls, "How is it that she's acquainted with the treasure map, Father?"

"Each generation of Bedouin searches for the treasure. They believe it will free their people, but much blood was spilled over the ancient map. Lilee hears these old legends from the oasis children." Father turns his head, nodding slightly in my direction, "Reportedly, the Bedouin have hidden the blood map."

"Measures are available to convince the Bedouin to reveal all." Mother smiles slightly, and thinks, *my old friends, the Coterie, are very appreciative of any treasure information.*

I smile inwardly that Madame does not realize how close she is to the map hidden in my blouse pocket; I don't understand her "measures."

"Enough of these fanciful legends and the bloody parchment. Marital arrangements should be a thing of the past," says Father softly returning our conversation to marriage.

"Do you want her to be on InterSocial when it comes to Farafra?" asks Mother sarcastically. "I understand women shamelessly interrogate suitors on that new courting show."

Changes POV

25

"These are new beginnings for women," explains Father. "The atmosphere is becoming increasingly choked and nature is at war; it doesn't give young people time for long engagements."

In the makeshift oasis school, the new pollutants are discussed daily; it's just another subject to me but the Inter-Socials will encompass our desert if Sam has his way.

"Lilee, Lilee," Mother says using her most subdued voice, "marriage to our family is of great magnitude . . ."

"Madame, she has options," interrupts Father. "She could learn to manage our farm."

Abba calls the small oasis business of local Bedouins, makeshift machinery, and a few friends who Father flies into the desert oasis—"the farm."

"Choices? Choices? Choices?" The wrinkles on Madame's brow multiply like father's pregnant hybrid plants, as she shrills, "They would never let her run our family estate. Marriage is the proper choice. Stay far away from the Commandant, Lilee, for your very own well-being."

Diverting my eyes from Madame, I freeze, unsure how to respond.

"These are solemn times," states Abba as he retrieves a chunk of bread. Then breaks, dips, and offers me the soaked piece, "to the future."

Confused, I take the morsel of bread. It is tradition that the broken bread was passed to the next of authority.

From his pocket he produces a thin golden ring and slips it on my little finger.

Madame's face explodes, "Father. Do you know what you do?" Her painted porcelain face hides beauty once coveted by many admirers. By contrast, her words sting like a viper's tongue. I fantasize that she could work for a circus because she moves easily from one of her personalities to another. "Father! Answer me. Do you recognize what you did?"

"Yes. These are new times. Challenging. When I die a new champion is required to fight the pandemic." Then he turns his attention to the haze over the plot of newly irrigated land framed in the many small windows. "What is to become of our land, our dreams?" Standing abruptly, "I must check the Twin Beach for my dawn departure." He strides from the great Hall mumbling, "Black Haze, you don't know who you are dealing with . . ."

"Foolish old man," Madame storms from the great Hall, "you're always dying."

Father originally plans a short trip for supplies which he can ill afford. But now, with the increased threat of the InterSocial on his research, he recognizes the need to extend his mission to include a search for backers. Time is not on his side. It concerns him that his absence would leave Lilee alone with scheming Madame and this beguiling Samman. *He is a dangerous man*, thinks Father as his Twin Beach gains altitude. *If only my brother, Jeune, and I did not exchange insults so long ago. He could help sort out the InterSocial and Samman.*

How does she Lilee know what he thinks?

27

Seven

Since she didn't quite promise Lilee continues secretly meeting Samman evenings in the Roman graveyard near her Qasr. With all his callousness I, Sparrow still don't fathom why she is drawn to him.

 "You're a romanticist," pokes Samman, shading his eyes from the hazy setting sun. "For idealists like you, there is no room in the new world."

"I have my loves," I say leaning thoughtfully against the coolness of an ancient headstone. "My father, my home, my Creator."

"You likely misunderstand. I mean you, Lilee of the White Desert, Farafra oasis, hold grandiose notions of the earth. You believe every marvelous thing was created for good. Through rosy goggles, you peak at the outside world."

"NO, I see clearly," I retaliate. "Oh, and let me add a baby to my love list . . . preferably a son. I would shower him with tenderness. He will grow gentle and strong. Could become king if we had kings."

"A child brought into the world," he says annoyed, "is subject to the atrocities of our current regimes." *This girl, Lilee, could be a potential pawn in our plan for world dominance.*

"Our oasis home is peaceful. The Bedouin love us," I smile. "Unfortunately few outsiders visit our oasis," blinking dust from my eyes. "You are the exception, Sam."

"I am Samman, *Samman*."

"Sam, you'll always be my Sam."

No longer able to temper his exasperation, "You're an ignorant child who understands nothing about life and the world outside this limited hellhole, Lilee. In the real world, we prefer automobiles and flying to riding horses." Alarmed by his intensity I step back. Seeing my uneasiness, he quiets his voice. "I am part of an elite group which will implant a device into your flesh by simple tattooing. One will have a choice of tattoo designs. You might like a flying sparrow. Anyway, this little jewel will update you 24/7. Information is power. So now your father can check the weather before flying, or where you are and if you're safe. The government can deliver medical attention immediately. This will give you trust and confidence to go about your everyday oasis life. Understand?"

"So, then you and your friends can follow us? Wherever we are? Where will they hide our freedom?"

"You're so childlike. Lack of your so-called 'freedom' is a small price to pay for what you get in return. The government will keep you safe . . . Oh, I don't know why I'm talking to you. You're too naïve. Spent too many years living in a broken-down fortress with an out-of-touch old man."

His words sting. *I'd never heard an outsider speak so violently against Abba.*

"You simple child. In the end, the Coterie—the real power in this world—will be the ultimate authority."

"Father provides the only authority I need," I say. "And will they regulate my tears, my happiness? And what about love and marriage and childbirth. Do they control that too?

"Marriage. Love. It's unnatural, a mere custom meaning nothing."

"What about children?"

"We recommend the sexes join up to reproduce when the bloody rank-and-file needs replacing. In fact, we're working to advance a modern method to procreate without sexual union. Something beyond intrauterine. The mind is involved. Experimentation is taking place as we speak."

Unable to find the words to refute his wildly absurd proclamations that seem to be menacing my world, I hesitate, "How can you speak so horribly of love?" Fighting back the tears, "My Abba, my Arabian stallion, my heavenly Abba who made me. I love them all."

"Love. Too simplistic an ideal. I don't know what it is," shouts Samman. "You play at love. Those you speak so highly of have no authority and surely don't love you."

On this moonless night, I stomp on his boots and run home.

Eight

Flapping vigorously, I fly into the inky sky, to find the person I once was. An unknown force pulls and I glide unsteadily to earth. On our last evening together I recall that Sam doesn't accept my belief that love is the food that nourishes me.

"You have told me virtually nothing about yourself," I say, twirling my hair between two fingers. I am met, once again, with his usual distant look.

In the overcast twilight, Samman's ruggedness complements his height. To say he is handsome is a guess for a girl who has met few men other than the Bedouin. He does not wear an official uniform of rank, only his fatigues, sun-bleached commandant's cap, and polished metals that exude military as if it were perfume.

We share a moment of silence as darkness closes in. Poised between two crumbling Roman columns in the cemetery, his stature is regal. Tall, strong, indomitable. It is then I know he is my prince. *Your words sometimes hurt, break my heart, but my love will change you.*

"Lovely Lilee. Lovely Lilee." He rolls my name into an aura of blistering heat, which sweeps up my spine. "In a few days if all goes as planned I'll be gone."

"We've so little time together." The high temperature vanishes. "Can't you extend your stay and count more Bedouin for your silly devices?"

"Perhaps if I stayed longer you will reveal some of your father's and this oasis' mysteries." Reflecting off his military metals the setting sun momentarily blinds me.

"If you are a little nicer I'll tell you the biggest secret." To block the dying sun, I raise my hands.

"So you admit there is some skulduggery at the oasis." Roughly he pulls down my hands and glares.

Regaining my composure but still shaken, "Of course, certainly Farafra hides many surprises."

He twists my hands. "Sam you're hurting me. If you love me you wouldn't."

"You wretched waif tell me exactly what your father is concealing." He squeezes my hands harder.

"Stop. You're scaring me." I yank my hands away staring at the bruises.

"Confess or suffer the consequences." He raises his right fist.

"I love you, Samman, really. That's the gigantic secret." I step back and he slowly lowers his fist.

"Love?" He turns to face the last rays of the dying sun. "You throw this emotional thing at me, a soldier, Commandant. Where does it come from? Your Christian God?"

"Yes, of course, Yahweh created us out of love." Still shaking, I confront him by moving to block the sunset.

"There is no such thing as love. It's as much a myth as God."

"Whom do you believe in?" I tremble more.

"Bloody well not a master puppeteer who hand carved us and pulls our strings." Waving his arms he imitates a marionette. "Then the master sends a Pinocchio to save us from ourselves."

"So you think a couple of desert crabs happened to bump heads making a big sound and our world," I move away to an eroded tomb and sit crossing my arms, "and creating pretty me." *Am I foolish to love this man who carries such anger?*

"More likely a band of she scorpions went on a rampage, my beautiful Lilee," groans Samman. "It's all random. I don't know why I am here. I've a lovely job to do. When it's over and my life is finished, that's it."

"Once you spoke of the beauty of faraway lands which stretched my young brain." *Sam calls me beautiful. Is there a little love in his heart for me?* "When I look at the grains of sand in our white desert, each is different and magnificent."

"You think like a child, wanting to believe all that is offered." He forces a smile, "Believe in me and yourself as a beautiful young woman who knows what is real by its touch." He offers his hands.

"I'm a young girl in a woman's body." I ignore his hands. Pausing to find the words which Abba taught me and my heart recognizes as true. "Ingrained in my cells, body and mind, is the longing to find my Creator who makes me as beautiful as you once described." Blushing I raise my voice to a loud whisper, ". . . and He is not a random scorpion. Truly I believe He is a person of great beauty and love."

Offering his hands again, he entreats, "Come away with me to the Americas and I will show you beauty, my love." Waving his arms he says, ". . . fields and forests of green that are bigger than your grainy desert."

"Need to finish my schooling. Can't leave my Abba."

"You are on the verge of womanhood; I will teach what you need to know, my love." *If only I hadn't chosen the Flags' vow of chastity. Perhaps we could have found love together. Anyhow, I'm confident she knows how the formula works. If she comes with me I'll force it out of her. It'll be easier manipulating her than her father.*

"And I'll teach you about my God." I stand stretching to my best height.

"With our feet stirring the dust of the dead in this godforsaken cemetery, you philosophize about some distant god who doesn't concern himself about my well-being. And surely I don't care about him, the . . ." He pauses midsentence, "What's that strange and beautiful sound?"

"It's a lonely desert cat howling. You seem so fearful about the possibilities of a Creator." I challenge him with my eyes. "Look at all the wonderful things like a desert cat, He provides. Even in the White Desert, He gives the magnificent power to our oasis, which sustains my family. Abba's frankincense and myrrh trees are nourished by His water and wind." I reach for Samman but he moves away. "I don't believe desert crabs or scorpions or any haphazard gestures would provide as much for me or my family."

"If you need a divine person, I can fill his boots," he says puffing his chest and rattling his medals.

"I can't forsake Abba and, besides, we don't see eye to eye." Samman wraps his arms around me in what I anticipate to be a parting hug, perhaps more. I raise myself on tiptoes and lift my face to his. I melt into him, welcoming his embrace. In an instant, a stinging prick cuts into my neck. Confused, I look into his eyes. A cold surge spreads through my body. I only remember my legs crumbling and Samman's leering eyes.

Nine

Fluttering my wings I can't peer into the windowless room as black as the darkness I came from. Why has Samman hidden her here in the family Qasr for the last nine months?

 Such pain, but beauty in the pain. I don't know what I'm supposed to do. I only know I'm exhausted. Drowning in my own sweat. Jesus, Mary, and Saint Nicholas the aching never ends. Thank God for the midwife crying, "push – ah. Push, push – sh."

How is it that I'm pregnant? Read about babies, never was with a Bedouin or Samman. Sam! The needle in my neck. Did you have your way with me?

Sweet Jesus, save me from the agony and that awful Samman. My eyes are on fire. My belly is bursting. I close my eyes to bursts of colors: crimson, yellows, and purples. And then a hint of sound quiets my pain.

A tiny whisper: my child is speaking to me.

The midwife lays something upon my belly and light seems to radiate from him. He chirps. A wondrously beautiful single chirp becomes a magical symphony to my ears. She moves him into my arms. It's almost unreal like watching a movie.

Instinctively, I place him to my breast and he suckles. I rejoice as my life ebbs into his, nourishing his very being.

From my pain comes life and beauty. My hurt no longer consumes me.

The midwife protests that I must eat. How can I leave his warm touch? I must protect him at all times.

In this windowless room, my son and I will live eternally, Prince and Queen. My mind is clearing with each passing day. A flickering light bulb reveals the colorless, peeling walls. Instead, I imagine tapestries and jewels surrounding us.

Itching, I grab long strands of threadlike hairs draped around my arms. I don't have long hair.

"Don't pull the nanotube fibers from the machine," shouts the midwife, panicking.

"What are they for?" I start to ask about the fibers, but a sharp knock interrupts the film I watch of myself nursing the child.

A silhouette holds the midwife while another brutally removes the gold ring from my finger. They grab my son from my breast. Instinctively I reach up and pluck something from the air. Red locks of hair fall between my fingers.

He doesn't cry. Is my baby alive? I am too weak to fight. My mind turns dark.

The symbol of my father's affection, a simple golden ring, is taken by these thieves. My little boy, a symbol of my life, stolen. Shocked and cold without his little warm body, I am no longer whole. Why didn't I cry out? Fight with all my strength? Without him, my room becomes a crumbling cold prison.

Another shadow moves toward my bed. A sharp prick to my neck reminds me of my last encounter with Sam. My fighting spirit dissolves to where I desire nothing.

My thoughts drift to an earlier sweeter time. Among the blooming oasis trees, I enjoy Abba's stories of the smiling Jesus gently gifting him a golden moral compass. I laugh that I am too short to see over the rim of his spiritual compass, but I remember how he secured my future spiritual home.

Gravely ill with childhood measles, Abba sprinkled me with the juices of frankincense and myrrh and pronounced the name of the Father, Son, and Holy Spirit. The fragrant liquid ran from my forehead staining his shirtsleeves like dark blood. I think he made a deal with God and dedicated me for some good.

Before my son's theft, I didn't have the presence of mind to baptize him with my sweat to save him and to consecrate him for something worthy.

Samman were you the one who confiscated my ring out of jealousy? Did you sexually assault me?

Desert cats chorus:

**From the murky waters
rises the blue Lotus
unstained, the Lily blooms.**

Ten

Excruciating flashes erupt in my Sparrow brain. It is all make-believe. The pain. The joy. Lilee is not pregnant; nor a mother.

 "Whore," shouts Samman. The midwife slinks into a far corner. "Where did you procure that horrible newborn to foil the birthing and the cybernetic baby created by the Coterie's machine?"

The terrified midwife twists into a tight fetal position in an attempt to hide from his anger. "I wished to comfort her with a real baby. Lilee is a mere child herself."

"I have a mind to ship you to a city where the plague is blossoming," says Samman. "Electronically induced pain mimics childbirth." Pointing to the midwife, "Lilee pulled on her electrodes trying to love that damn real child she thought was hers. Bloody fortunate my henchmen were at the door to steal away that pathetic infant." His face reddens, "Whose homeless waif did you steal?

Unable to answer, the midwife bolts for the door. The Commandant grabs her hair pulling her back and plunges into her neck a larger syringe of the same hallucinogenic drug used on Lilee. "Lovely, lovely, my superior presence plucked strands of your hair for Lilee to grab. Now she has a keepsake of your red hair which will force her to believe that she indeed gave birth to a carrot top." With one sweeping gesture Samman pulls another handful of crimson locks from the midwife. "My souvenir of Lilee's bondage to the Coterie."

Her pain is real, but when the midwife cries there is only gurgling.

Eleven

Clutching the Qasr window ledge closest to the door I shudder at Madame's cruel tongue. My precious feathers fly away to litter the desert. How can she do this to Lilee?

 "Returning from my unexpectedly long trip to keep our oasis farm from becoming a financial wasteland," emphasizes Father while pacing, "I learn you deliberately sent Lilee to a special finishing school nine months ago. Now you reveal she gave birth to a boy child. Is that despicable Samman responsible?"

Her back to Father, Madame stands straight, shedding his fury as an old snakeskin.

"I don't know if I should be more furious at you or Lilee."

An imperceptible grin washes over Madame's porcelain face. *The Coterie and Samman were most helpful in getting rid of my pathetic daughter. Their virtual machine is a marvelous creation. Imagine, she thinks she was with child. What a pitiful child, my Lilee.*

"While I was away safeguarding my future myrrh and frankincense hybrids," raising his voice which he seldom did, "you presented my illegitimate grandson for adoption before I laid eyes on him."

Madame's petite stature is coldly silent. Secretly she thinks, *a ramshackle back room in your beloved Qasr was her imaginary birthing chamber. Idiot.*

"Perhaps enrolling her in the Cairo Academy will bring Lilee to her senses and she will return to us with a proper education," says Father, struggling to control tears. "The girls' academy specializes in what?"

Madame stares through the multiple windows unaware of the shivering sparrow on the outside ledge. "Gymnastics and womanly tasks."

Turning, she glides out the Qasr great room. *My new association with the Coterie is quite profitable if I help maintain control over Lilee. This will teach you to pass my familial authority to your wretched daughter.*

Unable to fight back his emotions Father rushes through the fortress's massive doors, ignoring the fleeing sparrow. He seeks refuge in his frankincense and myrrh trees, perchance to water the new hybrids with his tears. "Concentrating on my struggling hybrid research it is better I never again see Lilee or her child. They are dead to me."

Twelve

Unlike Farfara's tranquility at the Academy she confronts toughness and strange girls. I shed sparrow tears. Will she ever be capable to "observe with her heart?"

Madame sends me faraway to a school in Cairo on the western bank of the Nile. It specializes more in clandestine curriculums than academics.

Near the end of the first month, a brown envelope is delivered by the oldest schoolmistress.

"Correspondence with your family is not permitted in the first year. Consider this your last contact."

The precisely written message is not Father's handwriting even though his signature appears on it: "If you aspire to be an assassin in life, you require the best training. Daughter, you will learn to kill in many ways. Some are not very pleasing. You learned your first lesson. You killed the love I had for you in my heart."

At the Cairo Girls' Academy, my grades are poor, but I excel in the martial arts. Tahita or "stick dancing" is my favorite Egyptian combat art. In quick figure 8 loops, I can flail a short stick which raises welts across my opponent before the swishing sound reaches her ears. I delight in raising welts on my schoolmates' arms and chests because they're anything but friends. These macho girls are groomed to be the female CEOs of a new breed of companies.

My second love is photography or what remains of the ancient magical film, especially the workmanship required to develop pictures. When I'm able, I borrow an old Lycon from a schoolmistress as old as the camera. Her words ring in my head, "one does not always see with your eyes; observe with your heart." I would then sneak into the desert behind my dorm and take imaginary pictures because film is scarce. She also provides my mind with philosophies different from the other instructors.

The Academy has the regimentation of a military school in the desert. During the first year of assassin training, I did not become proficient with a pistol. Whenever I tried to focus and shoot, my heart and hands trembled. And killing is another matter. Oh, I tell my teachers I am ready to kill anything in sight. Other students take field trips to closed museums to practice shooting. Fortunately on my outdoor trips, I was never required to slay any of God's creatures. I convince myself that when the time comes, I will annihilate with the best of my school chums. I attempt to surround myself with the toughest females who continually question my attraction to men.

"If you're straight like you say you are," they taunt, "you wouldn't want to be our friend."

"I like men," I fight back. "You androgynous lesbians are like Madame Bovias fighting windmills, but I still love you."

At the Academy girls aren't allowed jewelry, especially body ornamentation which has begun to fascinate me because I don't consider myself pretty. Quite thin with boyish features, I'm the tallest, emphasized by my straight black hair which I cut short in protest. Since I am not from a privileged family, groomed to be a CEO, the other girls only tolerate me.

To encourage our enthusiasm for martial arts, boys and their instructors from similar schools demonstrate at the Academy. These tough-faced males always want to talk. The little-minded men attract and repel me. They seem to have no beliefs, not even in themselves. Although they brag about the well-paying profession of assassin, I don't observe confidence in their pitted faces. Their instructors are no better.

My Abba exudes self-confidence. Without photos, his face is fading. *Does he still struggle with his experiments?*

Thirteen

Shaking, I flutter to the nearest Qasr window to watch. After many years Jeune returns to Farafra. From his youth the tell-tale sign of fibbing is revealed in Jeune's twitching hands. What evil lurks in the Coterie's hearts?

 Easing his bulk from the Jeep, Jeune takes a moment to survey Father's fortress, Qasr. In the orchards he notices the many young dried up frankincense and myrrh trees and shakes his head. *What choice do I have? Oppose the Coterie and face certain death? The sum of money offered for Abba's formula, if it exists, is not to be ignored. But how can I live deceiving my own brother?* Jarring the sand from his white wingtips, he shoves open the massive door.

Father slumps in the great room before an enormous fireplace from which several green glazed tiles have fallen. The dying embers in the fire pit cast shadows across his face, deepening the heavy folds.

"What has become of the pristine orchards?" Jeune looks around the room. "Your dwelling is a disaster."

Father responds in silence.

"Allow me to start over again. Greetings, my brother. Have I told you recently that I love you?" He hides his trembling hands behind his back.

"You, who are absent for years, express this deep affection?" Father stands slowly, shaking his head.

"Pray tell what pandemic has befallen your household?"

"Unannounced you appear at my humble oasis demanding answers. Why have you returned?"

"I'm your flesh and blood. From the sorry state of your estate, it's fortunate that I've come back." Jeune stares at his rapidly aged brother.

"Madame ran away." Forcing a smile, " . . . perhaps she joined her ludicrous circus." Swinging his arms, Father begins to pace. "Lilee supposedly had a child who Madame gave up for adoption. Then she exiled Lilee to a boarding Academy. I did not see either one before they were whisked away. My financial resources have dried up as have my hybrids."

"Abba, Abba. Your woes are like a bad movie. My heart reaches out to you."

"Do not use my name 'Abba'. Even though Lilee is 'dead' to me, it is a name only she can honor me with. Moreover, I question her pregnancy, especially when it comes from the lips of Madame. That scoundrel Samman must be the father. They all disappeared."

"Your name 'Abba' will not cross my lips. I do not have explanations to the mysterious stories of Madame, Lilee, and Samman." Jeune lies hiding his twitching hands and thinks, *if only I could ease my brother's pain by sharing the truth especially that his daughter is not a mamma.*

"Have you returned to torment me? When you disappeared, pulling your support from the oasis farmstead, you left harsh words on my doorway. Farafra may have missed you but I don't."

"Brother, I did not expect such a cruel welcome."

"Jeune, I judge you from your past words which were often shallow and deceitful. I need clarification for your unannounced appearance at my humble oasis."

"On my long absence, I was on a quest to benefit you and Farafra. Your humble estate is in shambles." Through the windows, Jeune scans the shriveled trees. "I left, if you recall, because our oasis business was not self-sufficient. I didn't abandon you. I went abroad searching for financial backing. Today I return on a confidential mission. One that serves to benefit you, my dear brother, if you agree to bend as an olive branch in the desert wind."

Father observes Jeune's exquisitely tailored, pearl white suit, raven tie, and shiny white shoes. "You appear at my door looking more like a used camel salesman than the former English professor. And one with a fake British accent. I hardly recognize you. Loosen your tie. Sit. Pray tell the scheme you have concocted."

Jeune's face reddens. *The bloody Coterie convinced me to adopt a fake British accent—it's part of their Coterie identity.* He hoped to ease slowly into his proposition and regain Father's trust, without which his mission from the Coterie would fail—Abba will never admit to the existence of the formula. *Obviously, my brother has no mood for my charm.*

"I'll get right to the point—from the current conditions of your oasis business you are on the verge of financial collapse. My research confirms what I see. It is my love for this magnificent land that brings me back." He waves his arms as a maestro to drive his argument. "I was abroad searching for backing from the Coterie. They are redefining history with their shrewd business practices and have taken special interest in Farafra."

"Jeune, if truth be told, why are you here?

"As you've probably heard, the Coterie desire to expand the InterSocial coverage globally. Farafra could be a key hub to broadcasts into the deserts." And Jeune thinks, *better to receive payment for your land and research than to have your work destroyed.*

"Are you in bed with these jackals?"

"No, no absolutely not," Uncle hides his hands. "After studying them for many years, I've come to bloody well appreciate what they can bring to governments and businesses. If you take me back as your partner, I will negotiate a splendid contract to buy more trees, irrigate the land, and renovate the Qasr."

"You mean, become like the Coterie jackals who I hear are manipulating the metropolises and, conceivably, the very air we breathe. Before submitting to the Coterie as you have, I would nourish the White Desert with my dry bones. I have no tolerance for the Coterie. Our family has honor. Do you wish to tear us from the pages of history?"

"I am definitely not an associate nor have I ever been one," says Jeune, pleased to project false sincerity. "Through my investigations, I've come to understand the Coterie and their manifesto. In many countries as the majority governmental party, they maintain stability instead of political chaos—especially from our current pandemic . . . I could go on and on. They infiltrated the InterSocial, corporations, and schools. Their influence is immeasurable, like stars in a desert night. But their primary goal is to rid the plague circling the earth. You've heard of the Black Blizzard. Whatsoever is happening in the atmosphere, causing sudden deaths all over the world, is of great interest to the Coterie. The Flags . . ."

"Wait. I've taken notice of the Flags and their bizarre religious customs. How are they involved?"

Jeune hopes to avoid discussion on this aspect of the Coterie. While members of the Coterie present themselves as strong businessmen, *few realize they are all Flagellants, better known as "Flags."* Their control over the InterSocial allows them to downplay their eccentric religious practices.

"If you remember, the Flagellants were driven underground, but it is they who established the Coterie which grew into the powerful organization it is today."

"So the Flags launched the Coterie! Is their bizarre religious belief the driving force behind it?"

"No, no. Well, yes." Jeune wipes the sweat from his brow with his trembling hand, unsure how to explain the Flags and their leadership in the Coterie without turning his brother completely away. "They blame the pandemic on mankind's sins and claim man has angered God. However, that doesn't preclude them from researching a remedy."

"Jeune, I sense there is more than you are revealing about their religious traditions."

"Decidedly, yes. But keep in mind, what I'm about to reveal refers to the Flags of years ago." Jeune secretly acknowledges, *this unorthodox behavior is still fundamental to their religious beliefs today, but practiced in private.* "At one time they did not bathe and wore the same clothes over and over. Sexual contact was forbidden. They marched in large groups with drums announcing their arrival. Each man whipped himself until he bled. Reports are their blood ran in the streets and splattered the crowds. These zealots are now a minority in the Coterie. The Coterie majority simply tolerates their rituals."

"You are inventing stories as you did when we were children. Show me your hands, Jeune. If they are not trembling, I'll know you are not lying."

"I'm not so clever to invent such a bloody group of individuals," Jeune finally admits hiding his hands. "Today the Coterie is a pragmatic group, able to separate religion and business. And one issue they are determined to conquer is the end to the pandemic."

"What does this have to do with me?"

"Brother, my dear brother. Rumors proliferate that hidden in the roots of your frankincense and myrrh trees live ingredients to combat the Black Blizzard."

"Ah. You think I have developed a formula at Farafra and you covet it. What has the Coterie promised you?"

"Tell me, Brother, whatever you've created, the Coterie will reward you handsomely if it is effective. My compensation will be to oversee the project and assist the Coterie in bringing a cure to market."

I, Sparrow scrutinize Jeune's fabrications to his brother. With age, deceit has become his only way to stay relevant in the new society. It has never been more evident than watching him stand before Abba and mislead him. What he did not reveal to Abba is that the Coterie has no interest in treating the Black Blizzard or healing the effects of the pandemic. The Coterie covets the potential formula in order to destroy it and any capabilities it may have. Their blueprint allows the pandemic to flourish and destroy agriculture. This opens the door to synthetic foods the Coterie will manufacture and the population will demand.

Not willing to believe there is not more to Jeune's interest in the formula, Father launches into one of his stories.

"Jeune, I cannot confirm or deny I have what the Coterie want. I do remember, however, that our grandfather's grandfather would describe this atmospheric phenomenon as a dust bowl of the 1930s. The American Great Plains states experienced a seven-year drought turning the land to dust. These vicious windstorms were called the Black Blizzard. Our grandfathers' grandfathers' soil was useless; just as our present air is becoming inadequate. A Black Blizzard grows over . . ."

Jeune heaves a great sigh. "Tell me, brother, do you or do you not have the solution?"

"This Black Blizzard condition is serious and I've taken steps with natural plants to solve the dilemma. In very ancient times . . ."

Exasperated, Jeune stands, "Are you delivering yet another history lesson?"

"Throughout the ages," Father, ignoring Jeune's question, instructs again. "Myrrh and frankincense have been valued for their dietary and herbal benefits. My chemists and botanists use the properties of each individual species to create a new product, nutriceuticals," smiles Father, thoroughly enjoying the lecture.

"Your jolly good friends are raised to the status of chemists and botanists?"

Through the windows, Father stares at the rows upon rows of struggling hybrid trees. "My associates are extremely competent entrepreneurs. The challenge is to extract the enzymatic substances from the hybrids." Father observes Uncle's blank look, but he pushes on. "The processed herbs could potentially slow down the absorption of the disease caused by the Black Blizzard, and even possibly provide a cure. As an awfully interesting byproduct, the prescription creates a rare perfume."

The Coterie will applaud my progress, and reward me handsomely, Jeune thinks. *Now I need to obtain the actual formula.* "If I understand you correctly myrrh and frankincense hybrids fashions a bloody exotic perfume. Survivors may be more interested in masking the stench of dying." Uncle's eyes twinkle. "My brother, there are profits to be demanded if you indeed have the 'recipe' to slow the disease. Just imagine your Roman garrison, Qasr, with its over 100 decaying rooms restored to its original grandeur. This land could be transformed into a Farafra hybrid plantation. The Coterie conglomerate will pay a king's ransom for your cure. And only the Coterie has the resources to distribute your formula worldwide."

"Jeune, Jeune. Agriculture is drying up. Natural food is not easily purchased. Even in our isolated oasis word has it the Coterie flood marketplaces with artificial foods. They are lining their pockets with Credits. How is it you don't speak of their treachery? Or is your head in a viper's hole?"

"Brother, you are wonky. Your bizarre theories are unfounded."

"I am certain the Flags are afraid of my formula and will destroy it in order to flood the markets with costly inferior synthetic food, only available ultimately to the rich. And, dear Jeune, I believe they bribed you to retrieve the formula."

"Preposterous. Brother, you are beginning to sound like the Flag fanatics, trumpeting their lies in the marketplace."

"Jeune, review the facts. In the parts of the world where the pandemic is concentrated, victims show swelling in their armpits and groin area, as large as oranges. Purple and black blotches quickly cover their entire body. Death soon visits these victims. If the disease doesn't kill them, starvation will as they cannot afford the Coterie's synthetics."

"Wrong. You are wrong. You give too much credence to rumors. In Cairo, I have dined with many Coterie and they are bloody good men who will help mankind."

Jeune searches his heart. Until now his greed hurt no one, or so he thought. Now, to his growing despair, he faces his brother and realized the truth. The Coterie overprice their synthetic food. His countrymen are deprived of nutrition. *Will they also be robbed of a possible cure to the Black Blizzard diseases?* A surge of true remorse overtakes him which he is not accustomed to feeling.

"Believe what you must, Jeune. My friends who work on the hybrid pharmaceuticals recount the shenanigans of the Coterie. They are the old Mafia dressed in contemporary camel shirts. I could never trust a Flag or their boss Coterie to safeguard the formula. And from the look on your face, I see you are beginning to have doubts."

"If the infamous Flags and their Coterie are as evil as you say, what would it take to oppose them? Knowing you, Brother, you've designed a battle plan."

Abba laughs and laughs. "Oh, you transparent twit, Jeune. You're going on the assumption I have a working formula, which you've been finagling me to reveal. Now you want me to share a battle plan? You think we're comrades in arms? You may have doubts, but you still work for my enemy."

"If you oppose them, your life will be worthless." Brother faces brother. "The Coterie will send their most experienced, dangerous, and cunning assassin."

"What will that accomplish? If I am killed, how can I hand over the preliminary unproven formula? So Jeune, leave. Tell them a cure is being developed. That verification should keep you in their good graces."

"Without admitting to anything, what would you say if I offered to collaborate with you?" Jeune coughs up his most sincere voice, even disregarding his British accent.

"I'd wager you are still deceitful."

"You're mistaken." Though shaken Jeune plays his part well. His love for Credits supersedes all, even his love for his brother. Yet he hopes to help his brother without hurting his own profits.

"Then prove it. Show me if your hands are shaking."

Jeune holds his hands very still. "Brother, you don't have the time to be obstinate. Your formula will die along with your trees in the desert if you don't have the finances to rescue them. I understand your distrust, but allow me to negotiate with the Coterie. They have unlimited funds like the sands of the White Desert."

"No, no absolutely not. You don't listen," responds Father. "The tentacles of the Coterie must not strangle our Farafra oasis."

"Then, with your blessing, allow me to pursue other financial support," appeases Jeune. "We must protect the formula from your enemies."

"The only enemy one has in the desert, if you are a big eared mouse, is a horned viper," smirks Father. "I can't say I trust you or your strategy completely. What is the alternative? My prize hybrids are withering." He forces a smile and nods.

"Truly, you have no inkling of who sneaks into the desert ready to pounce on your research. They would burn the Qasr down to find the blueprint, torturing your Bedouin in the process."

Pointing to his head, Father says, "The preliminary formula is very safe; it's not written down."

Jeune's confidence dissolves into fear bordering on a true terror. "If they learn you are the only one, they'll locate you and cut off your head. Your life is now worthless," and he thinks, *the Coterie will assign their most experienced, astute assassin.*

"At this moment you are the only other one to know the pilot formula's whereabouts. Whatever greed is in your heart, I hope that you are not a traitor to your blood brother."

In an ideal world, as a double agent, Jeune would retrieve the formula, give it to the Flags, collect a pat on the back and pocket an enormous sum of Credits. His brother would live. He would live. All would be well. But this is not an ideal world. His brother could be killed. He could die. The plague might cover the earth.

"Presume you've recruited a battalion to guard you and the formula which is funded by a not very profitable herb farm," grins Uncle.

"The troopers are you and me," sighs Father. "Fearful of the approaching Black Blizzard my research associates fled."

"There is another profitable path to explore brother," Uncle's eyes squint. "Years ago you wrote that the desert people entrusted you with a secret map. As I recall it showed the buried location of the lost Wise Men's caravan of gold. The Magi gold could be the alternative financial solution to safeguard and proliferate the hybrid formula production."

"Merely a legend, the Bedouins fought for years over an ancient bloodstained skin map. In the end, they found nothing and reluctantly handed it over for safekeeping. Since the map has the potential to instigate more hostility, I destroyed it." Without blinking Father watches Uncle.

"Foolish one," Uncle's eyes blacken, "you threw away the simple solution to save your hybrid farm and fight the pandemic hysteria. The precious gold would purchase a magnificent research team to replace your ragtag friends." He reflects, *gold is better than Credits in my pocket even if I must share some with the Coterie.*

"The map burnt brightly; I cannot undo it, Jeune."

"Somehow I don't believe you would obliterate a treasure map, but you have your reasons and, as always, they are a mystery to me." In desperation, Jeune adds, "If I become an agent for the Coterie, we would know their comings and goings and be one step ahead." *I'm so clever.*

"Ha, my brother your mind is not capable of thinking like a spy. Get out of my sight. Find a miracle to save us." With a single gesture, Father removes a small ceramic container from his pocket and sweeps three fingers into its sweet contents. He attempts to place his hand on Uncle's forehead, "With divine frankincense and myrrh I anoint . . ."

"Get that oil away," shouts Jeune waving like a drowning man. "Stop. Vulgar."

"My little brother, aren't you interested in improving your odds of finding a miracle?"

"I'll be back with a solution better than a miracle." Jeune bellows rushing out the door.

Fourteen

Ha, Jeune thinks he has problems. The Academy tile roof is not the easiest to hold onto with claws. I remember her curious encounter with her archetypal energies: Queen, Lover, and Warrior.

 At the Cairo Academy, the bullying increases. The less I speak the more their minds search for rocks to throw. There is no corner to hide from their stabbing jeers.

An old schoolmistress provides some refuge with her concern. "What is this talk of voices?"

"At night the wild desert calls."

"Lilee, you are searching," she says softly.

"My friends, they push and threaten."

"No one makes friends at the Academy." Her steely eyes convince me this is the truth. "This training institution does not encourage the improbable."

"But, but isn't it natural to want . . ."

"These evil creatures you desire to befriend will eat you alive with their morning sweet cakes," the mistress smiles.

"I'm ready to jump off a mountain. Where's the highest peak?"

"Lilee, Lilee delicate Lotus blossom, you are seeking answers outside yourself. First, you must look inward to find your archetypes."

These arch-o-types must be some psychological mumbo-jumbo that the school promotes, I ponder.

"Every woman has within herself everything she requires." She looks around to see if my classmates are near, "There are at least nine archetype energies within women which effect who we are. Yours are probably out of balance."

Before I could seek more explanation, a gong announces the next class.

The next day after training the old schoolmistress announces my assignment, "Practice shooting water lilies in the lagoon behind the dorms. And go find yourself."

Twirling an imaginary ancient revolver like the sheriff in one of my father's novel, the toughest females back away as I strut towards the evening desert. Parting them like the Red Sea, I hold my Tahita stick above their heads with my other hand.

There is a feeling I will meet someone in the desert and I break into a run. The sands swirl around and ahead.

Unexpectedly a hologram of a statuesque catlike woman appears with outstretched hands. *I freeze. Is she the felines of my dreams or a Queen?* Confronting the figure, I see my own now regal face and blue eyes. The Queen is me with my black straight hair. I want to run but am drawn to this powerful figure. My exhausted body slumps onto an ageless rock outcropping.

Closing my eyes I feel the Queen is one of my archetype energies. I long to find a place where I can be myself but am fearful of the journey. With trepidation, I follow her out of the darkening desert and into a bright garden in which light and dark shimmer through the canopy of trees. The wind plays among the wild grasses, mingling with the sweet lilac blossoms. My shoulders relax and I caress the gnarled trunk of a cherry tree pregnant with buds. The dark moss on the trunk has a feminine, velvety touch. Behind, in a grove of yellowing forsythia, a flock of chattering sparrows turns my attention to my inner feelings. Only in dreams in which felines sing to me, have I experienced such harmony.

I walk serenely to the shore of a clear blue lagoon and sense it hides my sacred place. My black martial tunic falls to my feet. The faint outline of underground caves shimmer in the water, beckoning.

My Queen archetype whispers, "Be fearless and confident."

The water is deep, but I am not afraid. I dive through the mirrored surface, creating the tiniest of ripples. The bubbly water massages my naked torso like a lover's fingers. Down, down I plunge through the ripples of my mind. As the caves become clearer I see they are the rooms of an underwater castle. Entering the castle's grand portal I imagine myself standing in a dry courtyard surrounded by walls of the finest stone, similar to my home in the Qasr. The castle has nine rooms with stained-glass windows overlooking my lagoon. Walking to the end of the courtyard, I open a short door and stoop to enter the first room.

The intimate chamber is overflowing with silky pale fabrics. Pushing my way through the delicate smoothness I come upon another catlike figure facing the softly patterned wall. Sensual music overwhelms my feelings, opening me to the beauty. Without seeing her face I listen to my heart and know it is my Lover archetype. She will not look at me because I realize I have not known love. An image of my mother abandoning me appears in my mind. Next, I observe myself as a teenager chasing after Abba. Wanting to kiss him on the cheek. Unable to catch him. I sense my Lover energy will not turn around unless I somehow change.

"Open your heart first to yourself and then to others," exclaims Lover over her shoulder.

Inside the next room, a catlike woman with a golden shield and sword confronts me. She has my eyes, but with lavender hair instead of black. Her eyes burn into mine.

Her gravelly voice is gentle, "I am your inner truth and gentleness, which is the true Warrior."

I do not fear her. She has come to free me. My heart leaps, singing like a sparrow.

Reaching for the archetypal Warrior's sword I awaken to find myself back at the edge of the desert. My right hand is grasping my Tahita stick instead of a sword.

Exhausted, I dress in my dark tunic which appears to glow white in the bright moonlight. *These experiences were authentic, and not a dream.*

There are more rooms of archetypes I couldn't explore. But the female energies I confronted will shape my future.

From that day on I vowed to apply my archetypal energies of Queen, Lover, and Warrior. I will not be imprisoned by the school or any of the students it manufactures.

Fifteen

Through the airport window I spy Samman marching back-and-forth. My sparrow heart races as I recollect him manipulating Jeune, Abba, and especially Lilee as pawns in his game.

At the Cairo airport gate, Commandant Samman paces waiting for a Lieutenant Zagh. When he finally spots him weaving through the crowd, his annoyance increases at his casual stroll.

"Was the European union conference successful?" inquires Zagh. He reaches for the briefcase which Samman grips more firmly.

"You're bloody late. The watchword of a Flag is punctuality. Be mindful if you hope to drag your pitiful body up the ranks." Samman scowls. "To answer your concern, most successful. The union is anxious to sign a synthetic food contract if the Coterie guarantees certain conditions."

"Europeans are concerned about our production capacity. I know."

"No. I assured them of our unlimited manufacturing resources." Samman frowns at Zagh. "Rumors have surfaced again about a pandemic remedy. Last year I met with a herbal medicine man that intelligence claims developed a cure on his Egyptian oasis. There may be something there, but I didn't unearth any viable signs of progress."

"The Europeans really believe the pandemic is reversible?

Striding ahead Samman shakes his head. "You simpleton. The union accepts the epidemic as the new norm. The InterSocial is successful at selling the name, Black Blizzard. They are fearful however a potential antidote for the Black Blizzard disease provides hope. This hope reduces the market for artificial foodstuffs. Entrepreneurs and competitive companies will again focus on farming real food with the optimism of an improving environment. The Coterie must eliminate news of miraculous cures on the InterSocial and any possibility of a remedy itself."

Zagh takes longer steps to keep pace with Samman. "After your visit to Farafra oasis, Commander, do you believe this herbal farmer truly has a hypothetical cure?"

"Until my father, Baba, steps down from Supreme Commander of the Coterie, do not address me by that title in public. Remember my mission was to determine the like-lihood of a professor growing frankincense and myrrh trees for medicinal purposes. Neither he nor his daughter, Lilee, would acknowledge a prescription, only some progress in hybridizing trees. Recruiting his brother, Jeune, to deter-mine the formula's validity, was not difficult with promises of wealth. More complex strategies are in motion to deceive his daughter, Lilee."

"As ordered, Jeune is waiting in the airport interroga-tion office." Zagh points to the door. "What are the chances of a remedy apparently brewed from frankincense and myrrh?"

"Tittle-tattles, all lies, but they keep resurfacing. If there were a bloody formula our conglomerates would have developed it." Samman rams the door open, "Follow my lead."

Entering the interrogation room, they slam Jeune against a wall. "Shut up and listen," threatens Samman.

Grabbing his neck they attempt to raise Jeune's bulk into the air. As a caught fish he flails; his eyes bulge. "Keep up the theatrics and you won't survive long," promises Samman.

They relax their grip and Jeune gulps the stale air.

"This is not a discussion. I'm only going to state this once. You and your pearly white suits belong to us. Go back to your brother and this time get the truth. This is your last chance. If there is a formula locate and destroy it."

Trembling Jeune finally admits, "My brother keeps the rough formula only in his head. He'll never give it to me. And besides, it's not completely tested."

"You've waited this long to report? Are you playing both sides?"

"No. It's just I don't want my brother dead."

Samman considers this for a time. His smirk disarms Zagh and Jeune. "This plays beautifully into my plans. From his briefcase he pulls a picture of his father, Baba.

In awe, Jeune stumbles back, "Baba and my brother could be twins. His facial features of jagged nose, low cheekbones and even silver hair are remarkably similar to my brother's except the scar and goatee."

"Ah, from his youth father's trademark scar crosses his left cheek. Make sure your brother cuts a scar, grows a goatee and impersonates Baba, our renegade Coterie leader."

"My brother is no actor. Besides with his scruples, he'll never agree to the charade." Jeune turns white afraid they'll kill him now.

Again Samman opens his briefcase and removes several large bundles of Credits. "These will convince your brother. The Credits will finance finishing the formula and then his race for freedom."

"My brother was expecting me to return with a miracle." Uncle steps back his eyes bulging.

"The miracle is financing to complete the research. The miracle will be surviving when we send our finest assassin," laughs Samman, "to terminate your brother, the alias Baba. The miracle will be a fighting chance if he's shrewd and escapes across the globe."

Jeune wants to protest, but can't take his eyes off the Credits. *Brother will be most elated for the backing and perhaps reward me. But where will Samman find this clever assassin?*

"As a special surprise to you, your botanist brother's estranged daughter, Lilee, very dishy, I say, is critical to my plan."

Jeune attempts to protest the services of Lilee, but Samman whacks his fist into Jeune's chest cracking the fourth rib.

"Harnessing our latest intra-embryo technology I induced Lilee to believe she gave birth to a ginger child, a sprog. Left with a handful of red hair I tore from the midwife, Lilee became mad as a bag of ferrets," brags Samman. "When the redheaded child card is played she will do our bidding, even killing." Taking Lilee's gold ring from his pocket, "to show we are serious," shoving the ring at Jeune he laughs, "you might want to share this with your brother at the right time so that he doesn't reconcile with her."

Again Jeune starts to object. They both squeeze his throat harder. Gasping wildly, *who is Lilee to murder? Not her own father!*

"Another angle comes to mind," Samman whispers into Jeune's ear. "Purportedly the Bedouin believe in a Magi gold legend. Using their bloody so-called authentic map they supposedly dug up half the White Desert. Only ancestral bones were found. The Bedouin might have hidden this map to prevent more mayhem among their people. If you bring me this fictional map, I'll guarantee a bonus, a new Coterie position as our chief altar boy, and not unleash our assassin upon your brother." Laughing loudly they release their grip.

Samman commands, "First get your fat Hulk back to your brother with the miracle of the windfall Credits. It is his opportunity to live a little longer. Or would he rather have his head cut off and the formula poured out of it? I think not. Instruct him to hide out in the Temple of the Snows monastery in Tibet where my father went often to meditate some mumbo-jumbo. Order your brother to finish the formula quickly. If he doesn't, my stealth assassin will pounce not only upon him but you. When this master of death arrives at his monastery door," Samman laughs louder, "your brother better run, run to try to save his pitiful life. AND you better start scurrying to salvage yours."

Dumbfounded Jeune stares. *What choices do my brother and I have—death now or later? Somehow he must complete the research.*

"Secondly after your chat with your brother drag your pitiful Hulk to Mandalay. Prepare to dress the part as Lilee's Ballyhoo Man, Solicitor, Handler. Personally, you will deliver the instructions for each of her targets. For security reasons the victims are to remain ANONYMOUS even to you. Don't botch this job or you'll become her target."

Can Sam turn Lilee into a killing machine? thinks Jeune.

Samman and Zagh heave Jeune through the door. Confused and ignoring the slight trickle of blood from his mouth, Jeune pats dirt off his white suit while stumbling toward the airport gate. *Little do they know whom they are toying with. Brotherly love is thicker than oasis water. To hide in the monastery with a new identity as Baba, my brother will have to be extracted from his current life. Possibly I can fake his death.*

Meanwhile, in the office, Zagh gapes at Samman. "What skulduggery? Are you sacrificing your father, our leader Baba?

"The consequences of the Black Blizzard fill the pockets of our brother Coterie with billions in profit. If I squelch InterSocial broadcasts of a clandestine pandemic treatment and destroy the hypothetical formula itself, the Coterie will elect me Supreme Commander. Just to be on the safe side I'll spread the nasty rumor about Old Baba: He is attempting to pull the wool over our eyes by returning the Coterie to its original spirituality which shuns wealth. With my nudging, he is on an extended vacation in the Americas. If my father the old goat returns, we'll put him out to pasture." Samman roars rowdier, "When we dangle her carrot-topped child as a prize, Lilee will chase Baba not realizing that he is her Abba. If she executes her father she receives the prize of her imaginary son. AND a corpse must be exhibited to the Coterie."

"Wouldn't it be simpler if we killed both Abba and Baba now?"

"Recall your flag vow not to stain our hands with murder. As the Supreme Commander, the soul of the Coterie, I will keep us on the righteous road. Remember, 'flag' often and change your shirt frequently," thunders Samman. "Seriously, fortify my support with the brother-hood, return to your political comic profession in Mandalay, and get chummy with Lilee when she arrives. I don't trust her."

Bugger off, thinks Zagh, *the cheeky supreme want-to-be is wonky himself. He sounds like a blooming standup come-dian. Lilee's a naïve girl and couldn't kill a sparrow. Listen to me tattling like a bloody-lutely Brit.*

Sixteen

Perched on the ledge outside Lilee's Academy dorm I've come to accept my sparrow's body. Will she take on her tattoo as a symbol for good or evil?

 A tangible symbol is needed to distance me from these girls, this Academy. Forging the ancient mistress's signature on a pass, I sneak into the old district of Cairo and locate a forbidden tattoo parlor in a desolate alleyway. As I knock on the whitewashed door a small sign announces, "Dr. Sumcoi—Purveyor of Dreams." The doctor assures that an image was assigned to me from the beginning of time and I need not worry.

"Really?" And then ponder, *will my tattoo be a sign of the new Lilee?*

After many hours, a blue Lotus tattoo blossoms on my left breast. Dr. Sumcoi explains that my name, Lilee, is a corruption of the Lily flower, but my tattoo represents my initial evolution. Although, to add to my confusion, the water Lily is not a Lotus flower. Sometimes I think I have an overabundance of information rattling around my head.

The pain is too much for this new warrior and I pass out. In a dream, the Lotus tattoo blossoms into my throbbing living flower, which twists and turns into female shapes. The petals unfold into a tall Queen with my eyes. The blossom then twirls into a Warrior with lavender hair. My Lover archetype doesn't join the dance.

How I found my way to the dorm I don't know. The old mistress caught me sneaking back, took pity on me, and warned if I tried this again I would be expelled. Where would I travel since my family will not take me back? I want to share my tattoo with my only friend, the old mistress, but I realize I have lost even her. My reaction is to stare back like a cornered desert cat and not a fierce warrior.

That evening, lying in pain, I contemplate the dirty dorm ceiling. Today again I experienced three very powerful persons within me.

It both scares and excites me to understand I have everything I require already within myself. My heart and mind were opened to reveal inner archetypes: Queen, Warrior, and Lover. As a Queen, I have the confidence and power and vision to be one with myself and make my way. As a Warrior, I can be focused, courageous, and protect myself and others.

Who do I think I am? I'm not a Princess much less a Queen. What kind of Warrior am I who can't stand up to an old schoolmistress? I don't deserve to be a Lover. Abba rejected me; I abandoned my child.

The next day, in an Eastern history class, the instructor introduces a Confucian scholar, Zhou Dunyi, who spoke simply, "I love the Lotus because while growing from mud, it is unstained."

The more I consider being unloved and not pretty, I remember the Lotus which roots in darkness but rises above the water to reach the sunlight. My spirit can grow from the mud of materialism at the Cairo Academy, which is drowning me. Somehow I will progress into the God light, enlightenment. The more the Academy pushes its culture, the harder I retaliate. I don't know how, but I will break through the murky water of my experience.

Through many exhausting classes, I finally comprehend that perfection proceeds through many stages shedding flaws until the ideal is achieved. The first level, symbolized by the blue Lotus, is a victory of spirit over the senses. The white Lotus indicates the second level, a state of spiritual and mental purity while the pink Lotus symbolizes the highest plateau of perfection. In my world full of evil, Buddha and my Christian God coexist precariously. I doubt my ability to reach even the beginning blue Lotus level which my tattoo represents. It would be simpler if an angel would reward my spiritual level by pinning a paper Lotus on my chest.

Contrary to the school's Eastern history classes, the Academy preaches brutal martial arts to the new level of female captains of industry. For those of us destined as second-class working assassins, killing is highly promoted.

My classmates do not possess an ethical compass. In fact, their compasses lack a pointer for any direction. In my heart I rejoice with a poem:

My retaliation, a tattoo.
Painful. A victory of the spirit,
castigating the death culture of the school.
My left breast aches, bleeds.
Not the last I will know blood,
fascinated by its ebb and flow.
The Lotus tattoo wears me
triumphantly.

Perhaps I will reveal
the blue flower to my assignments
before I shoot.

My meditation is broken by a distant howl of a desert Lynx:

**from the murky waters
rises the blue Lotus
unstained, the Lily blooms.**

Seventeen

On the Academy rooftop I also am a lonely Sparrow. Jumping and turning I try to reach beyond my nightmares to recapture my inner strengths. Then one day her worst nightmare appears.

 "You cannot ignore me," boasts a visiting instructor surrounded by his followers in the competition courtyard. "You are nothing but a thin boy masquerading as an ugly little girl." He is rumored to be an up-and-coming leader. His silhouette and smell are as familiar as a bad dream, but his face hides behind a protective mask.

When challenged, a warrior does not question combat. As he begins to circle, I finger my Tahita stick. Reaching for my arm with his left hand, I see his stiffened right hand propelling his staff toward my face. Whirling away and then stepping closer, I swing my Tahita thumping his face mask hard three times. I imagine a crimson welt on his right cheek under the mask. Staggering in disbelief he lunges his stick toward me. Stepping aside I flail my stick across his chest many times. The red bruises shine through his cotton shirt. Slumping, he turns slowly shouting as his supporters whisk him away to the pavilion, "Christian lover. I am your Samman."

Through the settling dust of the dispersing crowd, the sparrow in me wants so to fly after him, *but I am a new*

Warrior. Standing proud, *Sam you took advantage of me when you drugged me. Should have killed you now instead of just bruising your ego.*

After changing quickly I race through the courtyard intent on seeking refuge in my room. There's Sam sitting on a courtyard bench with a bandaged chest.

"I should be very angry with you. Instead, I am pleased." He smiles with a penetrating look and my heart melts.

"My stick should have broken your ribs." My warrior personality stares back attempting to control my flushed body.

"From a rather inexperienced girl you have grown into a masterful warrior."

"If this is your attempt at flattery you need to go back to school."

"Where are those loving feelings you expressed on moonlight evenings in Farafra?"

"My feelings vanished when you disappeared from my life. Why did you rape me?"

Ignoring my accusation, "Beautiful Lilee, come away with me to the Americas and be my Queen." Samman realizes he's losing control of his emotions and thinks, *stupid lass. She believes we had a son together. What if she accepts my invitation? I have already cast her in the part of an assassin.*

"Sam, I don't trust you as far as I can knock you with my Tahita stick."

He ignores her use of the familiar, 'Sam'. "I am truly proud of the skills you have acquired at the Academy. Your Madame made a fine choice with this school."

"If I had a voice in the matter, I would've picked a university with a different curriculum." *How did Sam know mother exiled me to this miserable Academy? Since I didn't*

ted zahrfeld

*fight harder to save our son I'm too ashamed to question him
further.*

"You'll make a fine assassin in our new society. With my
anticipated new leadership position I can find you a position. In fact, I know where there will be a need very soon for
a very special assignment." *Thank the fates I wouldn't have
to dance around her imaginary motherhood and listen to her
mourning her virtual son.*

"Don't do me any Buddhist favors. If nothing else the
school has taught me to pull myself out of the mud and
blossom. Amazingly this school is finishing the foundation
that my father started." The Warrior in me fights back the
teary thoughts of Abba. "Have you visited my Abba at
Farafra? I do wish you would keep a watchful eye on him.
He's so forgetful when he's engrossed with his hybrid trees."

"Oh, I've fostered a special interest in your father. You
might say my associates will be taking him under their
wings." He looks almost lovingly at me. "I'm a bit envious of
your relationship with him. In fact, I find your use of the
name 'Abba' a bit too syrupy."

"Don't you have a special name for your father?" I take
advantage of the small crack in his military facade.

Sam doesn't answer.

"Then it is true you were issued instead of having a
papa." I smile.

Sam looks beyond me as if he's trying to conjure up his
father. "There was little affection between us. His name is
Baba which means 'wool.' He heads up a rather secret
organization which I'm sure you've never heard of. He's
pulled the wool over this institute and especially me." There
is almost the beginning of a dry tear in Sam's eye. "As soon
as I could walk he hustled me into a military school. I
suppose I should thank him because it was the beginning of
a difficult fight to where I am now."

"Then you didn't spend much time together?"

72

"When I was rather young at my mother's funeral we were in the same room with a few hundred of his business associates. He barked orders at me."

"Talk around school is that you're the heir apparent of the popular group called Cot . . . Coter . . . Coterie. What say you, lover boy?"

"Enough of these rumors and affection nonsense. Lilee you have warrior skills to hone and I have to beat more young men into fighters better than you." And he thinks, *if I allow she'd talk me into arranging a lovefest between Abba and Baba instead of killing them.*

"Deserting me again Sam?" *Just when I thought he had a heart behind his medals.*

Sam manages to retrieve several medals from his pocket and pins them on his bandaged chest. "My dear Lilee, you're being groomed for greatness." *I know I'm evil. What kind of Creator permits such evil in this world?*

Eighteen

When Lilee turns into a believer I, Sparrow reluctantly become one. This sparrow desires a soulmate, but all Lilee can think about is a profession. The Coterie recruits her and I shutter.

 After two years, the Cairo Academy pushes me out into the world. The school says they can no longer deal with my lotus tattoo and my beliefs they called "other worldliness." I think of myself as a Christian Buddhist. After being sheltered on the oasis and at the Academy, living on my own does not cultivate my progress to the next level of perfection.

Since I avoided being "tattooed" to receive the InterSocial (you get implanted at graduation) I have no access to any positions.

Working in a Cairo teashop, after rent and food, there are few Credits left for fun. My idea of entertainment is acquiring black market books. Employment skills were not a subject taught at the Academy. My resources dwindle to where it's difficult to even to feed a sparrow.

An interview letter arrives at my tiny apartment; the envelope has a tire tread across the address. I would have ignored the invitation, but the offer is on Academy stationary and includes an old-fashion plane ticket.

My curiosity and the ticket takes me to a nameless, snow covered airport strewn with disposable cups and decaying foods.

In the abandoned terminal three men in parkas interview me for the curious position of digital photojournalist. Expressionless mouths pepper me with strange questions. "Can you fire a weapon? Have you killed?" *No one except Abba and Uncle knew of my dream to be a photojournalist.*

Explaining that I shot many vipers and graduated with honors (I lie—Father killed all the snakes; school never gave me even a certificate), invokes not the thinnest smile.

Amused, I shiver in the borrowed parka. A faint, disagreeable odor rises from their sexless faces. Fortunately, they can't observe my cropped purple hair under the parka hood. I thought dying my black hair would give me some credibility as a professional.

They continue rapid fire salvos. "Who is your father? What is his nationality? His employer?" I don't remember all my answers, except that he was a biology professor born in the Americas. Recalling my father brings a rush of warm memories. How I long to be near him instead of quivering while confronted by these nameless faces.

The next set of interrogations is even more meaningless. I sense they know much about me already. Perhaps they are measuring my answers against their resources; they're testing me. The interview ends with polite nods. They only smile at my questions concerning employment responsibilities.

On the airport tarmac my claws are freezing as I flick about peering through different smudged terminal windows. Then I spy them, Jeune and Lilee's father.

"Jeune, why have you brought me to this desolate airport?" Father shivers.

"Be thankful you are still alive. The Coterie will soon send their plane to deliver you to the Temple of Snows in Tibet. Did you bring the materials to complete your research? And the Credits for when the chase begins?" Jeune glares from beneath his white topcoat with the ermine fur collar.

Father pats a worn duffel bag and smiles, "You really think the Coterie will send an assassin to pry the formula from my head?"

"They will do anything to squish your formula, but the Coterie are intrigued by the possibilities of it producing a profitable perfume."

"Why not just kill me and Baba?"

"Their religious beliefs prevent them from committing murder. Instead, they will hire a killer who would not spill a whiskey while decapitating you."

"That still doesn't get rid of Baba."

Samman convinced him to start a small business in the Americas. Once you are eliminated, the Coterie will believe the real Baba is dead. The road to Samman's takeover as Supreme Commander is secure." Jeune wraps his top coat tighter. "Your only hope is to complete the formula or run like hell."

Father is stunned.

To lighten the impact, Jeune adds, "the Baba-like scar on your left cheek appears genuine and your goatee is growing nicely."

"My cheek bled long when I cut it. Will I fool anyone that I'm Baba?"

"You, my brother, need only fool your hunter. Are you sure you have everything you need to refine the formula?"

Father slaps his duffel bag.

"At the monastery, concentrate on the details. A perfected formulation will be a negotiating term to save your life," lies Jeune.

Again reaching into his bag Father removes his lady liberty Glock. "This weapon won't do me any good. Give it to Lilee. She may need it for protection."

"I'll give it my best to locate your daughter." Then he thinks, *how will you respond when confronted by your daughter, the unthinkable executioner?*

"One more very important detail," he extends a chubby finger, "since you disappeared from Farafra we need to make it more plausible by faking your death."

Father jumps up, "Killing me off already. Exactly how?"

"Don't worry I'll take care of the details," says Uncle sitting Father down and reflecting . . . *to make it more believable, I'll marry Madame.*

Alone on the flight back to Cairo, downcast by the interview, I stare at the big "F" emblazoned on the next seat, but not noticing below the word "Flag Inc" in small letters.

In two days a courier delivers an old fashion envelope. Ripping it open I read an offer of employment for the position of InterSocial digital photojournalist. Report for training . . . I don't know whether to laugh or yell for my disbelief is greater than my joy.

Arriving at an abandoned factory in a neglected part of Cairo, I regret not researching my prospective employer. Explaining to the anonymous welcoming committee that I have no photojournalist credentials, they assure me the InterSocial wants a fresh approach with a new voice. I will be provided with a shutterless, continuous focus, digital camera. Their experts recommend I teach myself by shooting any newsworthy incidents. *At least won't be shooting victims.* After heated, but polite discussion about Credits, I am proud to say, I accept the position.

It is then they calmly extend an old Chinese pistol saying, "As a digital photojournalist, you might receive a dangerous assignment in a politically unsettled metropolis. Consequently, you will require expert training in its deployment."

I sense trickery. My warrior archetype kicks in. With a red face I shout, "You want me to learn to shoot?" Standing as tall as I can, I ask, "At who? I didn't sign up as a murderer. 'Dangerous assignment?'" Raging at the thought I was deceived. After exhaustive discussion, they reassure me they have no dangerous tasks in mind. To appease my doubts they will not implant a communication device, but instead provide a classic wearable medallion. Again they promise that I am being groomed for a special assignment in the future. Most of my time is to be spent in self-training and observation. Reluctantly, I accept their reasoning. *At least my childish dream of being an assassin will not become a reality. Besides Abba never liked my assassin idea.*

"This ancient revolver will misfire and kill me," I argue. They agreed to locate a reliable Glock. *Abba's hands were very rough as he taught me to shoot his Glock.*

Training is a farce. In the makeshift firing range I repeatedly score few marks within the body chart much less the bull's-eye.

In other classes, I am bombarded with InterSocial media hype. The most interesting class is an old-fashioned photographic how-to. "Don't see only with your eyes; observe with your heart," is repeated often. These words are a familiar echo of my old schoolmistress. The phrase smells spiritual, which seems unusual for this materialistic business. I'm not sure how to apply the dictum to my photojournalism.

Because they do not have a facility, they recommend I pursue more martial arts training for additional protection.

"You will receive your assignments in person through a short pudgy man who always wears expensive suits. He is your 'Ballyhoo Man.' Remember him well."

Questioning the term "ballyhoo," they inform me it means my manager, solicitor.

After two weeks, they proclaim I have graduated with distinction. "Honor?" I question. Their reply is a cheap diploma and a polite round of applause, which fans a sweet aroma covering some mischievous odor. As I recall, the secretaries, clerks, trainers, and managers are all men.

In this graduation class I am the only one.

Well, it's good to have a career, a profession, and thank God, not as an assassin. Deep in my mind I bury the contradictions of my training and the burning question, *what is my special assignment?*

Nineteen

On the upper plains of New Burma, which is old Myanmar, her employer sequesters Lilee in Mandalay in a modest loft to await the first assignment. I, Sparrow am very happy for her. The weather is beautifully warm.

 In one day an old cargo plane transports me to Mandalay. It's a step back in time. Today, I stand in the streets of the Burma police state as if it were the twentieth century. The authoritarian political system is unchanged. On street corners, the Imperial police proudly wear their retro 1900 khaki jodhpurs and polished black boots.

My spirit is refreshed by the sounds and sights of Mandalay. I love to say "Mandalay"; the lyrical sound tickles my tongue. Open-air teashops spill the aroma of strong Typhoo tea. Bazaars tempt my senses: Turmeric, garlic, smoked fish and anise. A masquerade from the past whirls in front of me: street dancers, silk weavers, jewelry makers, puppeteers.

My first task is to gift myself the cat I was denied in my youth. It is not difficult to find directions to the animal shelter in the biggest bazaar, Zaykyo. The shelter is a zoo of exotic and domestic animals. Through howling and cawing I fight my way through surges of faceless browsers. In a back corner, a bamboo cage filled with tortoiseshell marked cats sits in an oasis of silence. They are as oblivious to me as they are to the menagerie of discordant sounds. Staring at each of the nine felines, I hope to connect. It is a test of wills. The cats are winning. A short plump brownish tortoiseshell catches my eye for a brief second. Over time and space, I feel an ancient connection with her. Responding to this instinct I ask the shelter attendant to capture her into a basket before I change (or she changes) my mind.

Hurrying with my prize to the front of the shelter, an indefinable urge causes me to abruptly turn. A tall, rather thin, reddish tortoiseshell feline is locked on my gaze. Her feverishly green eyes penetrate deep into my soul. There is no fear, only a joyful calm. Neither my feet nor mind want to respond. Only when the basket slips from my grasp do I snap back to reality. Dragging the attendant back to the bamboo cage I feverishly motion that I want the second feline added to my basket. The shelter manager would not negotiate a price for the two cats other than my promise to volunteer at some future date. It seems that tortoiseshell cats are not prized in Mandalay and he was happy to be relieved of these burdens.

As I return to my loft in King Thibaw square, I inhale the paradise of tamarind trees and flower gardens lining the entrance. When my hand strokes the teak gateway I think, *isn't it ironic? In a police setting hides a visual Utopia. Bravely to the rest of the world, it touts a false democracy.* Although I am not free I am creating my own Utopia with my feline companions. My thoughts wander across lists of names for my only friends.

Perched on the facade four stories above King Thibaw square I, Sparrow, question their feline intentions. During Lilee's yoga meditations at the Academy, tabbies often starred in her dreams licking their whiskers. In the past, she believed the cats watched over her. In her present situation they may be her nemesis. But, then again, her Queen, Warrior, and Lover archetypes appear with catlike features.

Waiting for my solicitor, "Ballyhoo," to deliver the equipment necessary to my new profession is a bit tenuous. Instead of martial arts, I decide yoga classes will improve my personal lifestyle and relieve my tension.

The next morning, I locate a yoga class in the old section of Mandalay. Attached to a high-energy bar is a short modern building; a flashing red neon sign proclaims, "I Kiss You Yoga." As I breeze through the heavy glass doors I squelch a laugh. The Yoga trainer resembles a retro movie star, a thin Space Cadet. His yoga costume is luminous red, stretched tight.

"Here for the training or meditation?" his deep brown eyes flash.

"Meditation."

"Experience?" he purrs like a lion on the prowl, looking me over.

"None," I lie.

"Join the other wannabes," he smiles provocatively, motioning towards the other five youngish Asian women in colorful high-end yoga wear, all trying not to glance at my slightly worn black sweats. I offer a "hello" and receive a mixed response of greetings.

The yoga session is an exhibition for Mister Cadet. He has us hold positions while he ogles our female features. During my cobra posture, he has the audacity to whisper in my ear. "Arch your back harder. Thrust out your breasts. Whoops. I mean chest."

His stares divert my concentration from my breathing. Also, Monkey Thoughts persist: flashbacks of Father sitting in the Qasr courtyard ignoring me.

Sweating I give into my frustration and anger. When the two-hour session ends, I hurry to be first out the door.

Mister Cadet catches my arm, "Would you like to share a pot of tea or something stronger?"

"Not really dressed for any sharing. Let's have supper at the Burmese Russian Tea Room."

His eyes are on fire, "Marvelous, but there isn't a Burmese Russian Tea Room."

"It's newly opened," I lie, "in Mandalay square, next to the bazaar." *I really love the sound of "Mandalay,"* I think and then smile. "At sundown, handsome."

"Perfect."

Pushing through the door, I avoid his slap on my thigh. Climbing into the first available trishaw, I compliment myself, having diverted this pesky bee from my flower. I laugh in the knowledge that there is no Burmese Russian Tea Room. As quickly as it began, I end my training at "I Kiss You Yoga" center. To compensate my loss, the Mandalay sights, sounds, and delicate smells, wrap me in joy.

Twenty

Now that I am a sparrow the felines look at me differently through the window glass. They may be my archenemies. My spirit wants them to be my angels. They fill a void in her heart.

 The first month in Mandalay is lazy, idyllic.

I have no camera or assignment. Left to my own devices, I grow weary with exploring the mysterious Mandalay. Over my freedom, hangs the dark shadow of my solicitor. I wonder when Mister Ballyhoo Man will appear. Mockingly, I give him the proper title Mister to his codename. Waiting in my loft to kill time I name my tortoiseshell cats.

"You, plump cat, look at me."

She gazes at the sparrow on the window ledge.

"First it is difficult to name a cat and a challenge for two—you and your tall friend."

The taller feline also looks intensely through the window glass.

"A feline has two different names. There's a name I will give you both that makes sense to me. Tabby or Phantom. Old-fashion common names. None of these titles seem to fit. The other name is the secret names only you, my cats, know and will never tell."

The felines look at each other and grin.

"When I see you both in quiet contemplation, *although tortoiseshell cats are known to talk incessantly,* I believe you are thinking of your own special names."

Together the felines begin a melodic chorus.

"Rather wish you would contemplate my concerns: my first assignment, the whereabouts of my firstborn, my Abba, and the lost gold. But you are of no help in these weighty matters. Then again you are felines of ancient Egyptian heritage or so swears the shopkeeper from whom I rescued you." I touch the hidden treasure skin in the pocket over my tattoo.

A spring shower interrupts my musings with its wet fingers skipping across the window. Following my cats' rowdy purring I watch a drenched sparrow hop out of sight. "Shush, the poor thing has no home."

"After much spirit searching, plump cat, I name you 'Lover.' Truly you love yourself but open your heart to others."

Turning her head, Lover looks over her shoulder, sensually raised up by the dignity afforded by her name.

"Your friend the tall one I will call 'Flower.' The ancestral Flower was companion to the fourth Magi." Turning to her I say, "As a warrior, you are strong, yet gentle. Hopefully your strength and courage will shine on me."

Flower stretches royally.

"Indeed, in one legend, Flower carried both the dagger and blood map."

The felines commence purring in unison.

Fatigued, I collapse into sleep. In a dream, I see Lover and Flower swaying side to side as they intone a refrain. Whether awake or asleep when my felines invade my thoughts I rub my blue Lotus tattoo. In the first stage of my life journey, I have accomplished little. Their chorus echoes my possibilities.

ted zahrfeld

Over and over again in my head, they sing:

From the murky waters
rises the blue Lotus
unstained, the Lily blooms.

Twenty-One

In the beautiful hodgepodge of Mandalay's motorcars and bazaars I observe a bright political comedian contrasted with a dour Ballyhoo Man.

 After weeks trapped in my loft and besieged by troubling dreams, I starve for nature. The peepul trees are budding and the bougainvilleas are flush with vermillion blossoms. The Black Blizzard has only lightly touched New Burma. This morning wears the haze like a net scarf. By afternoon, most days are bright and intolerably hot. Previous wars and fires demolished most of Mandalay nestled on the great Irrawaddy River, bordering the Republic of New China. Chinese Credits and entrepreneurs rebuilt the inner city. Gaudy steel and glass buildings contrast with gilded pagodas.

On the way to Zay Kyo, the biggest bazaar, my afternoon walk is spent dodging merciless motorcars, motorcycles, and bicycles, not to mention the ever-present trishaw.

From an old woman street merchant, I buy a small yellow bud for my hair. She offers tree bark rouge and says how nice the flower crowns my cropped lavender hair. With much misgiving, I cut the ebony hair my father gloried. My new glories are ravaged short and streaked to make me look worldlier. I take the vendor's compliment but refuse the Burmese cosmetic.

The bazaar is a maze of multicolored garments dancing among stacks of exotic produce, vintage antiques, and black-market goods. Water greens, gourds, and eggplants are meticulous bedfellows alongside mangoes, grapefruits, jackfruits, chickens, shrimp and dried fish. The abundance fascinates my simple Farafra mind. I grow claustrophobic with all the pretty things I want but can ill afford.

To avoid buying, I wander back toward my loft and stumble upon a black-market bookseller in an alleyway. To call it a shop is a misnomer. The remains of a discolored parachute are spread on the roadway. An avalanche of books tumbles across the floor. Many of the books are in languages I don't recognize. Twentieth century, well-worn novels share the piles with damaged textbooks and leather bound classics.

Sitting on the floor the proprietor in a crisp linen shirt hides behind the mountainous disarray. He resembles a nervous peddler who is ready at a moment's notice to fold up his pack of books, and disappear into the crowd.

Without looking up from the Dickens' *Ye Olde Curiosity Shop* manuscript, he greets me in a comical British accent, "Whatever you're looking for we dodgy well don't have."

"Shakespeare," I ask, ignoring his comment. "Nicely bound."

"Tragedies or comedies?" He still doesn't look up. "Sonnets," I emphasize in my sweetest voice.

"Out of stock. Backordered," he answers, jumping to his feet, discombobulated. "Sorry beautiful lady. Taking care of this shop for a friend."

"Seriously, any Shakespeare?"

"Not much call for the Bard," a twinkling smile lights his strong face, "since the last literary bonfire."

"Book burnings in Mandalay?" I ask cautiously.

"Public burning on Monday nights, 8 to 9 p.m. Free admission if you donate a book," he laughs. "Only jesting. I'm the up-and-coming local comedian. Name's Zagh."

"Are you a comedian moonlighting as a bookseller?" I play his game, "Or are you a book pirate mimicking a comic?"

"A lover of words," Zagh says lyrically, drinking me in with his deep dark eyes, "and other beautiful things."

Our banter is interrupted by a large commotion of scattering street merchants.

"Imperial police," shouts Zagh, bundling the books into the parachute cloth and disappearing in the opposite direction.

"Wait. I'm at King Thibaw Square. Bring the Bard," I call after him.

The fear of being arrested keeps my back to the increasing noise which sounds like a battalion on maneuvers. The marching stops behind me.

"Please to set eyes on smashing Miss Lilee," roars a familiar voice with a touch of broken British accent.

Turning, I'm shocked and relieved to witness a short, dumpy, and neckless hulk in an exquisitely tailored, off-white suit, and maroon tie. A large canvas satchel drapes across his chest. "Uncle Jeune? Are you on holiday?" I ask sarcastically.

"Ballyhoo," he whispers.

"Uncle, Mister Ballyhoo Man?" I blurt and resist snickering. *This is a bad movie.*

"No name, use no name," he whispers, sounding more like a movie character, and motions to follow him to the teashop across the alley. He tries to grab my hand but I resist. Uncle is not my favorite. He was gone most of the time when I was growing up. Besides, he has become as huge as a mansion, perhaps 300 pounds. I remember how Abba loved that word "perhaps."

In an empty corner of this busy teashop, we sit on wobbly wooden stools facing each other across a long, narrow wooden table. Mister Ballyhoo takes up the entire length of one side. He appears to have absorbed his wooden stool like an enema and I fight giggling.

"Tea," I say politely to the anxious waiter.

"Right, right," the hulk commands.

I explain I am not hungry, but he orders the biryani, an Indian curry rice dish with prawns which he inhales. Fried parts of shrimp litter the table. Nausea is surely to be my next best friend.

"Uncle . . . ah, Mister Ballyhoo," I sip the strong tea. "Why are you my manager? Have you reconciled with Father?"

Ignoring my questions, Mister Gourmet drops the satchel with a loud thud into the remains of his meal. The other Myanmar tea drinkers stare, but quickly turn away when they see Mister Hulk. He is like a grotesque Santa Claus about to open his sack of goodies, but Uncle is not as benevolent.

"Tools of your profession," declares the hushed voice, slowly unzipping the canvas. I peer into the black interior. His huge hand delicately lifts a playing card sized silver box. "Camera. A very special camera. No focus. No shutter. It takes many, many pictures digitally."

"You'll teach me?" I enquire, fearful he would merely hug the camera to smithereens.

"No. You're a professional. Go into countryside and practice. Shoot, ha-ha, many, many beautiful pictures. Store everything electronically. No connection. Zip, zip through air. But you can never see images," he beams, raising a paperback-sized box. The black box, I gather, is the computer of sorts which stores the images.

The hulk in front of me is no longer my uncle. He has gone through a transformation. I'm undecided whether it's good or bad. My insides are churning as particles of food continue to fly from his mouth. Undeterred, Mister Santa Hulk digs deeper into his sack and slowly brings a metallic object to the brim so the inquisitive tea drinkers can't observe.

A Glock, I whisper to myself. Feeling a little better, even safer, now that I possess my hard negotiated weapon. Peering closer, I recognize the worn Lady on the handle. *Father's beloved Glock.* "How did you . . ." A warm feeling flushes my neck and breasts. "Is Abba dead?"

"No questions. You are a professional under orders," he interrupts. "As this is a special occasion," Mister Santa says, raising a vintage Ralph Lauren midnight black linen pantsuit. "You like?"

"It's beautiful!" I secretly wonder if he's trying to buy my loyalty or the suit is a gift from Abba. "How did you know my size?"

His look is austere. "The InterSocial knows everything there is to know about you, Miss Lilee, including how you do not comb your hair." He smiles. "They know your life history better than you might understand. Your father, Abba; mother Madame; your uncle; and you, lady Lilee, are an open book, if they printed books.

"Did Abba ask about me?" I ask frantically.

"Everything will be revealed in time," he motions me to lower my voice. "I can inform you your father is very alive and working on his secret formula."

I nod without expression. *Not sure I want to trust Uncle and acknowledge any information about Father. Wonder if he's near to a solution?*

"See the haze which the InterSocial calls the Black Blizzard," he emphasizes pointing to the outside blackness capturing the afternoon. "Since your departure, your humble father and his colleagues have come close to completing a marvelous pharmaceutical formula that attacks the heart of the Black Blizzard." *Let's see how much she knows.*

"You mean he and his tree pruners and tea drinking friends sprinkled desert doo-doo, while flying in Father's screaming Twin Beach plane," I grin and think, *Uncle doesn't comprehend the formula. It will not cure the pandemic only, possibly, relieve the resulting suffering.*

"In a faraway place, your father has gone into hiding in order to complete the compounding of a smashing hybrid of frankincense and myrrh." *Really hiding from you his soon-to-be pursuing assassin,* thinks Uncle shaking his head.

"My father doesn't have magic to stop the Black Blizzard." I punctuate the words slowly.

"Well, I'm not sure. Your father talks in stories. I believe he's saying his pharmaceutical has the prospect to ease the pain of dying. Maybe even prevent some deaths from the Black Blizzard."

"That would truly be more miracle than magical. Think of all the lives which could be saved. Political powers must be beating down Father's gate."

"Governments don't believe in miracles." Then Uncle thinks, *especially the Coterie infested governments which are more interested in destroying the formula whether it's viable or not.*

"But they will work with my father to produce this medicine quickly?"

Nervously, Mister Ballyhoo ignores my question and continues in an impeccable accent. "It is imperative your father's work be monitored for the greater common benefit."

"Greater good," I become uneasy. "Who is this 'who' will be watching?'"

Leaning closer, his garlic and curry are overpowering. "It is imperative you understand who your bosses are. Yes, you are employed by the InterSocial. They are the first layer, like the skin of an onion." I could see he relishes using food images. "And this *they* are not the real they."

"Yes, I know the InterSocial has replaced the old Internet; I work for them. You're not telling me anything I don't know," I interrupt impatiently.

Undeterred, Mister Gourmet licks his sticky fingers and I fight the returning nausea. "The core of the onion is the Coterie who grew out of the nasty Flaggerants. In fact, they are all blooming 'flags' as I affectionately like to call them." I wonder if his bosses would appreciate the sarcasm.

"I've heard of the Coterie but who are these Flags?"

"The Coterie cleaned up the Flags' image. The Coterie run the world. Without the Coterie, the bloody moon would not glow nor the sun blaze." Uncle is very pleased with his imagery.

"You are painting a picture of a secret society," I say rather hesitantly, "a secret power."

"The Coterie own the InterSocial and operate the Financial Institutions which converted the monetary system to Credits. They pull the political strings of most governments," he frowns unable to find a food analogy. Leaning even closer his huge face blocks the light, "The Coterie, in fact, has taken your father under their wing."

Uncle's broken accent has taken on a more impeccable tone. *Is Uncle a suave British agent in disguise or Doctor Ballyhoo Jekyll?* Regaining my composure, "How does my father or for that matter me, a bottom rung, digital photo-journalist, fit into this onion basket of Flags and Coterie?"

"My dear Lilee," he reaches for my hands, which I quickly hide under the table. "Your father is protected by the benevolent hands of the Coterie. By their grace, you are honored with a beautiful residence in Mandalay and I will eternally be your protector."

Somehow when he speaks the lyrical name "Mandalay," it sounds dirty. His actions disgust me, especially when he attempts to hold my hands. *Are his actions to reassure me? Or is he becoming too friendly? Where is a comical book peddler when you need him?* "What am I supposed to do in marvelous Mandalay?"

"Prepare diligently for the InterSocial's special assignment. Shoot extraordinary images. Go into the highways and byways and capture the least likely commoners."

Mister Ballyhoo Man is giving me a biblical mission. "When will you deliver the instructions for my special assignment?"

"In due time," he proudly adds, "there will be many preliminary tasks to prepare you. I will relay the projects. In the meantime, practice. Practice shooting *ha, ha, ha* with your camera . . ." The huge face breaks into a grin, "and the Glock. Bloody enjoy."

How could I enjoy being alone in a foreign country as beautiful as Mandalay? My agitated brain can't decode his words. *Was he prodding me to practice shooting more pictures or Abba's Glock?*

"The Burmese police will not take kindly to your camera or weapon," he cautions. "Practice shooting in the countryside, including the Glock."

"The Glock?" I wince, *never considered ever using a Glock much less Abba's Glock.* "Did you steal her?"

"The weapon is for your protection. Fortuitously, I was able to switch your father's Glock to replace the cheap model your employer procured. Your assignment may take you into dangerous territory where I may not be able to secure your safety."

His explanation does not clarify anything. Our modern society provides a high degree of security for tourists and us media gatherers. It's a matter of economics and profit.

"Where are these dangerous places I might be at risk?"

Mister Ballyhoo turns to frantically rummage through the satchel and his pockets. "There is one more very important tool," he hesitates, "which is temporarily misplaced. Tomorrow at dawn, we will meet in the King's Teahouse." To emphasize his control, he adds casually, "I neglected to mention your son. They know his circumstances. For the record does he have a name?"

"My son, is he alive?" I beg loudly and heads turn. His memory blurs my vision.

When I refocus, Uncle has vanished from the teashop. In the diminishing sunlight and increasing black haze, I catch a trishaw to my loft. Images of my baby son and unknown assignments agitate my hands as I press them into my lap.

Twenty-Two

Beginning to recall more sinister events pierces my spirit. Frantically flapping my wings I tumble from the roof of the teahouse. The pain of these memories is like childbirth.

 The sun is fighting through the murky dawn when I arrive at the teahouse in King's square. Mister Ballyhoo Man squats at a low table in a far corner. "I have taken the liberty to order myself mohinga, fish soup with noodles, and for you my dear, nanpiah, a flat Indian wheat bread. And of course Myanmar Tea."

I sip my strong tea in silence, trying to shake off the troubling memories of yesterday's meeting. Uncle is treating me as a stranger. *What is he concealing?* The thought of my uncle as a sinister agent brings a smile to my sleep deprived face. *And how could Uncle Ballyhoo double his weight?* His lifestyle must be most lavish.

Thoughts of the life that I brought into the world bring a painful ache to my heart. I wish now I had named him, but in the moment it seemed unimportant. Without a name, he doesn't seem mine. These agonizing thoughts are killing me. *My son probably doesn't know I exist. Can't he sense that his mother longs to see a face, to touch his red hair, to love him?*

"Take me to my son or else." *Time is running out to teach him all the good things my father taught me,* I think.

"After all your deep contemplation my child this is your command?" Uncle Ballyhoo gobbles his soup and begins to devour my flat bread. In disbelief, I stare at the amount of food needed to fuel this monster.

"Or I'll quit the InterSocial or the Coterie. Whomever I work for."

"Don't have the coordinates of your son's location. That information is guarded by the Coterie who may be disposed to share it if you follow their orders."

Uncle is nothing but a creepy agent, I think and throw the remaining bread at him.

From his pocket he calmly retrieves a small medallion. Gently placing the golden object in my hand, Uncle Ballyhoo lingers, holding my fingers. The object is a medallion the size and shape of my thumbnail. Although appearing to be gold, it is warm to the touch like amber. The embossed letters IS are intertwined with a serpent. I recognize the acronyms for the InterSocial. Squeezing the medallion produces more warmth as if it has a life of its own.

"As you are aware, all citizens," he states, "must wear or have tattooed an international communication device with which they connect to the InterSocial. It's all the media you can imagine and delicious entertainment." He pauses thoughtfully, "It's a two-way lane. Citizens have access to news and events as they transpire. The 'they' of the world track our every move whether it's across countries or into a shop down an alley."

"A digital photojournalist should have more liberty of movement to succeed in her profession," I huff.

"Yes, you raise such a tirade about dangerous assignments," he grins. "The InterSocial is providing you an older wearable device."

When I beat my son's whereabouts out of you I'll thrash this medallion."

"Careful, they have no sense of amusement," Uncle emphasizes. "Everyone is bloody wired and their instant experiences are uploaded to the InterSocial." His huge frame rocks in amusement, "Once I tied my device to a goat. The security police were not amused. My time in detention was instructive."

"A devil of a comic you are." Pointing, "If I had a knife I'd cut your heart out."

Becoming serious, he points to the medallion. "Embedded is a chip which allows the owner to be scanned as a P I N, 'Person of Interest None.' Lilee, you must wear the medallion at all times." For emphasis, he reaches to touch my hands which I draw back once again. "You will be recorded as a person, but not identified. Only an extremely important individual is permitted to be anonymous." His mood changes, "For your protection, the medal is to be worn when you bathe and sleep. Always."

I want to add amusingly, *And when being loved,* but I don't. *What's the name of that comedic bookstore vendor?*

"In our wisdom, however, you must provide how to wear it," he says, motioning with his arms as if to hug me around the neck. "I suggest you acquire a chain from a local shop."

Fingering the medallion, I ponder, *it is my St. Christopher's medal to move silently, safely. Invisible.* My face flushes with this power. "Digitally I can document a political upheaval or sudden death. Upload the images to the InterSocial. Sign it from an Anonymous Sympathetic Source, A. S. S." I don't relish calling myself an ASS.

A rush of footsteps distracts my attention from Uncle who disappears. He is replaced by the seated bookshop comic. In disbelief, I stare at his dark eyes and short raven hair which bolts in all directions.

"For a person his size, your guest vanishes fast. Can't quite recall me?" asks dark eyes, noting my surprise.

"You're the waiter from the alley tea shop," I tease.

"Probably my style, I'm not very distinguished as a comedian." His eyes and lips are animated with bright laughter.

To prevent getting lost in his gaze, I toy with him. "Aren't you the mayor of King's slums on the outskirts of Mandalay?"

"And you are one of the rogue comics who sneak across borders. Queen Lilee or is it Lilee the improv comedian."

Zagh knows my name but I didn't disclose it yesterday. Fear and laughter are strange companions, I think.

For reasons known only to my heart, this stranger reminds me of what I imagine my son would grow to become: sensitive, yet well educated. With a grand sense of humor. *Why do I torture myself?* He's like thousands of lost orphans who've not survived.

Tapping my arm, "Lilee, the InterSocial and local gossip, and your violet wig makes it relatively easy to identify you."

How much does he really know? I contemplate. "My employer unplugged me from the InterSocial."

"Everyone has remnants of their past on the InterSocial." *She is so fearful. Does she recognize me?* "Well, you might be more thankful that I saved you from a fate worse than Burmese water torture," he mimics in the direction of the vanished Mister Ballyhoo Man.

"Righto, Mister comic. It's my own hair and lavender streaked," pouts my purple glossed lips. "The huge man is a friend. And besides, are you really a legitimate comedian or are you here to torment me?"

"I'm Zagh, the inquisition torturer-in-training, at your service."

"Prove you're a comic."

"Dressed in a purple robe, Lilee climbs Mt. Popa in search of the wisest Buddhist. 'What is the meaning of life?' she asks him. He motions her to come closer and whispers 'broccoli.' 'We don't have broccoli in Burma,' she cries. 'Okay, mango,' the Buddhist replies. Disappointed, Lilee descends the mountain. On the way down, she stumbles over a cliff but manages to catch a branch while falling. Hanging precariously by one hand, she shouts, 'help, help me.' A voice from on high answers, 'Let go and I will save you.' Through her purple eye shadow, Lilee looks down and then up, 'Anyone else up there?'" Zagh spreads his arms, hooting.

"You need to find a real profession," I applaud, amused that he notices my eyes. "I definitely don't need saving." Then think, *but I do trust you and I would let go if you catch me.*

"Quite seriously," he wrinkles his brow and draws me into his eyes. "At the local tea shops, I was a political comedian. The authorities didn't appreciate my humor. After serving six years in prison, they granted me amnesty. Must keep my act socially acceptable," he laughs.

"Remarkably, bloody bad," I tease, mimicking his accent.

"Trust me." He slips his hands into mine and squeezes gently. "There is much political unrest in New Burma. The people were under totalitarian rule for decades. They live in poverty, in makeshift villages. Mandalay is my stage and I am the voice of the oppressed." His hands grow warmer as he speaks.

"Can you take me to a village?" I exclaim, thinking to myself, *it would be good practice.* "For a documentary. I've credentials as a journalist. I mean digital photojournalist."

"It could be dangerous. The people are not violent; they're only hungry and unemployed." He leans closer, "One never knows when there will be a political military sweep of a village."

"I'm willing to take that chance. My employer is the InterSocial. This could become late-breaking media." The revelation of my prestigious boss does not surprise Zagh.

"The worst village is on the outskirts of Mandalay, but we must get an early start tomorrow." His warm grip releases my hands, "Besides, I'm running late for an appointment."

"Can you recommend a trusted artisan who specializes in gold?"

"I have just the chap and his shop is nearby."

The rogue artisan accommodates me with a delicate, golden Circles of Life chain to secure the medallion. Trembling, I show him the few strands of my son's carrot top hair concealed in the folds of the bloodstained map. Cutting a thin incision in the back of the medal, this artisan surgeon embeds the strands and closes the wound. If I must always wear this medallion, my son's lock will be close to my heart. The medallion becomes my amulet.

Twenty-Three

Overlooking Mandalay, perched in a dying peepul tree, I observe her and Zagh sauntering to shantytown. What will she find in this village which contrasts with her family?

 The next morning Zagh insists we first visit the Royal Palace prior to the photographic adventure to the village outside Mandalay. My forest green Ainygi, waist length blouse which I wear over my Lungi, a floral print sarong, conceals the camera.

Hand-in-hand, he scurries me along, like a father anxiously taking his daughter to a Buddhist festival. We stop abruptly in front of the Royal Tea Shop.

"Fortification." Zagh steers us to an outside low table. "Typhoo tip tea, strong, not too sweet," he orders. "Tea is magical. It will lift our spirits for what we are about to observe. Some say it has the power to make one stronger and braver."

From where we sit, a spectacular view unfolds of the Royal Palace of King Mindon. Zagh explains that most of the Palace was destroyed by the British in the 1900s. "Some of the walls and towers survived and of course the moat. The reconstructed halls and pagodas are reminiscent of a more peaceful time when Burma was in charge of its own destiny." He points to towering gold leaf spires glistening through the morning black mist. "The magnanimous junta, as we affectionately call the State Peace and Development Council, rebuilt this edifice as a symbol of how times have not changed."

"Has anything improved?"

"The ruling military would like you to believe the story has a happy ending. In fact, conditions are worse, much worse, as we'll bloody well observe."

Grabbing my arm, Zagh hurries us towards the 30-foot high walls guarding the Royal Palace surrounded by several hundred foot wide moats. "There are many spies in tea shops," he whispers. "The military continues to grow in size, devouring the economy. The majority of the population eats scraps left in back alleys. The date of the popular uprising in the 1900s is still their secret rallying cry. 'Four eights' which stands for 8–8–88." He reflects, *it's easy to get close to her.*

Leisurely, arm in arm, we stroll past the Royal Palace, the massive walls cascading with blood red bougainvillea are reflected in the peaceful moat. *Lovers*, I think, *on a Sunday afternoon in old Paris.*

"Within the palace itself," Zagh explains, "a large military garrison is hidden under the magnificent golden domes where courtesans once danced for the king."

The contrast between the old and new makes my heart sad.

"The Great Hall which is open to the public distracts us from the hidden garrison," he says, leaning closer to slightly move my lavender hair with his breath."

"The past splendor of the Royal court and a proud people are better memories," I add, turning to stare into his eyes.

We walk silently through blocks of small shops until we reach the hills at the outskirts of Mandalay. Without crossing borders or a time zone, we're in another world. The colorful and plentiful merchandise of the shops are replaced by a black-and-white squalor

At the top of a barren knoll above shantytown, I stand petrified of descending into this hell. Row upon row of dwellings, if I can call them homes, lay arranged in a hodgepodge maze. A forest of huts constructed of bamboo, cardboard, discarded shipping containers, plastic, and unknown cloth, is woven together into nests and shelters. The shantytown unfolds at the dirty feet of the mountains.

"It's dodgy, but all right." Zagh gives me a quick squeeze around my waist and points to this phantom city mostly hidden by plumes of dark and light smoke. "These people have endured much cruelty, but they are not unfriendly."

Opening a crease in my Ainygi, I pan the stark scenery with my camera. It appears as the remains of a major bombardment. I do not want to go into this abyss, no matter how friendly the inhabitants. Satan himself and his band of carousing demons will surely jump from the nearest shanty.

Taking me firmly by the hand, Zagh drags me into this shantytown underworld. "Squint your eyes as you look at the dwellings," he offers, "they will not appear so harsh."

Heeding his advice, I stumble to the first makeshift hut. The open side of this cargo container is decorated with melted plastic flowers on a latticework of bamboo. An elderly couple guards an open cooking fire. "Light-skinned, tall Shans, most likely refugees from Cambodia," whispers Zagh. Wearing an old colorless sarong, the woman squats, stirring a pot over the coals. A young child sits between the man's legs in a hammock created by his tattered sarong.

"Saya, saya." Rising with the boy child, the elderly man greets Zagh warmly calling him teacher. Zagh whispers to me that the elderly man must have heard of him as a comedian, but mistakes him for a scholar.

Gesturing to my comic that I would like to take the couple's pictures, he asks and they nod in agreement. The man's face is gnarled with years of quiet acceptance. Destitute, but not broken. The deep furls of his brow and cheeks are cruel symbols of a difficult life. But beneath it all, I see a glimmer of hope. His toothless smile appears easily and often. As he adjusts his torn sarong, he is a king preparing for a royal portrait. I take numerous shots from different angles.

Dressed in rags, the boy child is surprisingly plump and angelic. My first instinct is to grab the child, hug him, and run. He could be my son. No, my son is older, but he could be hiding in this squalor town.

Shaking, I desperately look over the nearby dwellings overflowing with young and old.

Stroking my arm, Zagh whispers that out of respect I should also take pictures of the boy. Each shot of the smiling child escalates an overflow of motherly love for him. Reaching for the medallion, my amulet with my son's hair, I squeeze hard. My fingers are noticeably warmer and my spirit is lifted.

I study the elderly woman and recognize an elegance not faded by a hard life. Though withered, her face glows with inner warmth. As she stands stirring the pot, she has the ageless grace of motherhood. She turns her smile to me and I note nobility. I honor her by taking many more pictures. *Would I have been as good a mother?*

The frail couple offers to share their meager meal. I smile and Zagh explains that we have more homes to visit. *Why is it that those who have so little, offer it to others?* I can't even share copies of their images for their neighbors to admire. These elderly have no communication devices or access to the InterSocial. They are invisible, truly forgotten. Waving its magic wand, the Junta government wants them to disappear. I sense a kinship with these people. For my profession, I am using every method to appear invisible, while they're fighting for recognition and justice.

"Four eights," the elderly man whispers the guerrillas' rallying cry to Zagh.

Arm in arm, Zagh and I continue to descend into the depths of shantytown. We are voyagers picking our way through a surreal purgatory. I force myself to take pictures of the dwellings, which are starkly hopeless. The shanties cry to heaven in desperation, wanting to redeem their inhabitants.

By contrast, the faces of the dwellers are strikingly beautiful. Every line and pock mark speaks of optimism.

Simple things like meeting strangers provide enormous happiness. Hunger is their constant companion. Driven from the city, they pursue a little farming, selling, or thieving. In their most inner hearts they dream of moving into the city, into a real house. A job. The way these families treat each other and share their meager food demonstrates their compassion for one another. The shanty families are a contrast to my former oasis family. I begin to doubt even Abba's affection and ponder, *must have been the cause of all father's grief by luring Sam and having his child.*

"My senses are overloaded. It's a good weariness. Any longer and you'll have to carry me."

Zagh confides that he feels little love for shantytown residents because they deserve their destiny. Then he thinks, *must be careful not to antagonize my emotional Lilee.* "I know a shortcut back," he says, changing the direction of the conversation. "We'll catch a trishaw into Mandalay."

As we board the trishaw, I look back at squalor town. The black-and-white fearful hell, which I first saw, is populated with hope-filled families who don't warrant their fate. The expectation of recovering my own family is fading with the evening light.

Twenty-Four

While Zagh and Lileee go traipsing off to Bagan, I keep my claws on a solid window ledge in Mandalay. I don't trust Zagh. For a comedian without a soul, he's too charming.

 The next day at the King's tea shop, Zagh meets me early.

"You're a darn good soldier," he grins, "for suffering through that bloody lot of shanties. You've earned a special reward, one with splendid photographic opportunities."

After a brisk walk, we catch a dilapidated train for a short trip south to Bagan, on the banks of the Ayerarwady River. "The city of Four Million Pagodas," Zagh teases, but offers nothing else. Swaying and rumbling, the ancient train is held together with patches of army green, salvaged metals. Our coach is overflowing with red, blue and green sarongs, the smell of warm flesh, and exotic food aromas.

In Bagan, the historical capital of the first Burmese kingdom, we walk a short distance into the countryside dotted with temples. "King Anawrahta established the first capital by stealing the oldest Buddhist holy books," chuckles Zagh, "carrying them to Bagan on the backs of thirty-two albino elephants."

At a Buddhist shrine, we pause on the marble terrace. Its domes and half domes are topped by spires reaching hundreds of feet. I'm awestruck by the rich layers coating the spires. "Indeed it is gold," he explains. "Some chaps say the gold leaf is as thick as your little finger."

"Magnificent, fit for an Emperor," I grin.

"Or a queen."

"Rather be the Queen of Sheba," I tease.

"Marco Polo," Zagh breaks the spell, "the poor chap was enthralled by the golden roofs of Bagan. He bloody well thought they were made of solid gold. Interestingly the towers like spires of a cathedral appear to be monuments to a king. Some sort of spiritual significance."

Looking beyond the statues of Buddha, large bells, small prayer halls, and the late afternoon rush of scurrying worshipers, I see a landscape unfolding with more golden temples.

"A better view awaits us," he points to a nearby open field atop a low hill.

A loud hissing sound draws us to three massive globes rising like planets. Silver, blue, and red orbs hover above, tethered to the earth, each illuminated by the fires in their bellies.

"Never flew in a hot air balloon," I say with trepidation as he helps me over the waist high side of the balloon's basket. "Is this wicker contraption strong enough?"

"Safe, very safe," shouts a dark-skinned pilot from behind the gas flame filling our silver balloon. Rhythmically, he works a lever that forces the flame to leap into the balloon's expanding belly.

With one hand squeezing Zagh's and the other gripping the basket until it hurts, I gaze up into the glowing balloon. I imagine an upside down volcano crashing down and clench my eyes shut. The basket beneath my feet begins to rock slowly. "I'm going to fall."

"No. We're lifting. If you don't open your eyes," Zagh teases, "you'll bloody miss the experience of a lifetime.

Peeking out of the corner of one eye, I observe in horror that the pagodas below are receding, smaller and smaller. The many stone Buddhas and bells are becoming miniature toys. I cannot discern one statue from another. The temples' wood, alabaster, bronze, and ivory walls are melting together. Only the golden domes are visible as we sail towards sundown.

"Sunset ballooning," inhales Zagh, "more glorious than at sunrise. Are you going to photograph?"

I reluctantly release his hand and begin to shoot the landscape. Leveling off at about 500 feet, we float above what could be thousands of pagodas. The golden towers are set on fire by the setting sun. Thousands of spires surge golden flames, like fiery fingers throwing us to heaven. To my left and right, our two companion balloons are rotating red and blue warrior planets attempting to capture us.

In the small basket of our balloon, each time the pilot fires the burner, I feel the warmth of its flame embrace my cheek. The balloon continues to crawl slowly towards the horizon like a lover under a sheet.

At the mercy of the gentle breeze we inch onward at its beck and call. There is no sensation of motion. We are one with the air. The wind is us. One gets a false sense of security. Leaning over to take a better shot, I lose my balance.

"Careful, you are too precious a ballast." Zagh pulls me from the edge and holds me, "For you to fall would be such a waste." *Sweet Lilee, you are the star of the Coterie's play which brings down your father.*

There is a quiet serenity. Burying my face into his shoulder, we don't speak. Floating above the earth in the waning sunlight, two souls are suspended between heaven and earth. I feel safe in his arms, wishing it could last a lifetime. We are wrapped in the music of the twilight. Each passing moment is a decade of changing reflections.

ted zahrfeld

Looking down again I see the rapidly disappearing tapestry of purple, red, and gold pagodas in the fading light. *Why, when I'm with Zagh, do I even think of Abba? My hopes of seeing him are dying.*

Untangling myself from Zagh, I shoot the kaleidoscope of towers and spires parading slowly below us. I ask myself, *Is this what Yahweh enjoys when he looks down?* The temples may have been built to honor the Bamar king, but these towers are monuments to the Creator. *If I abandon hope what do I have?*

"See Mount Victoria?" Zagh points to a distant mountain. "It's 10,000 feet to the summit and, incredibly, there's a bloody pagoda on its peak."

The ebbing light, mirrored from the mountaintop temple, is a spiritual beacon, a newborn star.

As the air cools and the light kisses the Earth goodbye, we begin our descent to the slow whisper of hot air being released.

A gentle flutter of color lands on the basket rim. A bird-wing swallowtail butterfly. Almost eight inches across, she is striped in dark and light blues. My father delighted in knowing butterflies. I dare not move for fear of frightening her. *Is she a mirage or a sign?* Transfixed, I am absorbed by her fragile beauty. A minute passes before, mysteriously, the butterfly disappears.

"Swallowtails are common in the old world tropics," Zagh shakes his head. "I've only seen a few in Burma and never at this altitude."

"As a young child my father, the professor, told me a Roman legend," I sigh. "Cupid fell in love with a mortal woman, Psyche. She was told never to look at her lover. Curiosity got the best of her, she peeked, and Cupid fled. Endlessly, Psyche searches for her lover. Pitying her, the god Jupiter causes her to be immortal and she is reunited with Cupid."

"Very touching story, but what does that have to do with the gobby price of tea in Mandalay?"

"The Greek word for butterfly is 'Psyche,' meaning soul. Some cultures believe the soul of a dead person returns in a butterfly form. Butterflies symbolize rebirth, change." I think, *Father would have been proud of my remembering his lessons. Seems only last week that I sat at his feet, renewed in the warmth of his love.* "Do you believe in a soul?" I peer directly at Zagh.

"Not really, I'm not being funny, but beliefs like that aren't productive."

"What do you believe in my comedian?" I focus deep into his eyes, hoping to understand his "psyche."

"Mainly myself," Zagh looks up at the silver balloon tethering us between heaven and earth and not at me, "and a certain organization which I unquestionably support."

I do not press him further because I know he suffered by championing certain anti-totalitarian groups. Since we seem to be growing closer, I need him to understand my beliefs.

"Zagh, reincarnation is not one of mine. But there has to be something which makes us who we are. Soul is a special name for this spirit. Or would you rather call it cantaloupe?" I try to get a laugh, but his response is silence. "My soul spirit provides the capacity to re-create myself as a mother, warrior, and lover. Although I'm not doing a great job," I say, squeezing his arm. His lack of response troubles me and I wonder, *what dark secrets are hiding in his soul?*

As the full moon begins its ascent, our hot air balloon makes a soft landing near the mountains. After tethering the basket, we help the pilot deflate the balloon until the chase jeep arrives. Exhausted from the experiences, we ride back to Bagan, absorbed in our own thoughts.

"We have reservations at the charming Blue Moon Inn," Zagh interrupts the silence and thinks *must slay her spiritual side to free her to kill.*

"You are so full of wonderful surprises."

"Your sullen face contradicts your praise. A basket of Credits for your thoughts."

"Oh, Zagh would have loved to share our experiences with my dear father, but we are estranged."

"My connections may be of value should you wish to contact him."

"No, I only want to know if he's well."

"What if daddy was really bad—hiding some dodgy skeletons in the cupboard? Could you punish him?"

I start laughing until I realize he's serious. "Yeah, sure Mister Comedian, my Abba's a fabulous double agent. I bet you played a dual agent many times on the stage."

The conversation ends as abruptly as it begins.

The moonlight tickles and I sit up sneezing. My head pounds. The small room is cramped with layers of light. The air is heavy with the fragrance of human bodies. Lying in the canopied bed I touch my breasts, realizing I'm half undressed and not alone. *Where am I?*

I attempt to recount the previous day. After the ballooning event I recall us driving to the Blue Moon Inn, happily tired from shooting golden pagodas. Famished Zagh and I share a late supper of mango, papaya, and cantaloupe in a curry peanut sauce. Much laughter as I play with the dark sauce. His beautiful eyes. He's much older. Disjointed conversation. Much palm wine. My head throbs.

Zagh, did we? I don't think so. Too much to drink and I'm dressed. Not that it would make any difference. But it does make a difference to me. Zagh's a lot of fun. If he is to be a future partner, and the father of my other children, it should be something beautiful, meaningful. Zagh doesn't know anything about me or my son. *I want another child.* Thoughts of my son crash my reverie. He's a young boy now. *Is he handsome?* I think he's out there somewhere. *Hope, why are you deserting me?* Reaching for my amulet, I panic. *It's not there.*

Desperately rolling closer to Zagh, I search the sheets frantically. Finding the amulet under his shoulder I carefully grasp its warmth. Sighing, I run the golden amulet down Zagh's naked back. His strong arms are passionately wrapped around the pillow. The fragile comic. His sweet body fills my senses. He's more beautiful than I am.

Didn't have Sex. Make love. Do it. Whatever the hell you call it, I'm relieved, but I wanted to. Wish I had more experience with lovers but they would probably hound me like the Black Plague covering my body with their deadly kisses.

In desperation I dress in the moonlight. My Lotus tattoo is reflected in the dinghy windowpane. Silently opening the door, I disappear into the streets in search of the night train to Mandalay.

Twenty-Five

Oh Lilee. My pretty Lilee I see you falling into the same snare. Zagh is another candy cane man drawn to your sweetness. Or is he?

Weeks later in Zagh's Mandalay apartment, I curve into the soft layers of duck down. He strokes my shoulder, "Do you have a . . ." he nibbles my hair, "nickname?"

His words bring a coldness to my naked body and I pull the black silk sheet over my shoulders. *Sparrow*, I say to myself, *Father called me his little Sparrow.* I smile, then lie. "No, Zagh, not really."

"Too bad, will have to name you," he says thinking, *Killer might do.*

I turn away from his gorgeous body to gaze at the stark trees through the window and then at his walls. There are no pictures of loved ones, relatives or friends among his sparse furnishings.

Why doesn't he love me? We play like brother and sister under the covers. Has he been hurt in the past? I have grown accustomed to not being loved.

Perhaps putting distance between us will create some jealousy, I think then make up an assignment. "I must go to Vorarlberg, Austria tomorrow and shoot the mountains and Tibet to shoot the monks.

"Will the authorities clear your passport?" he offers then thinks, *is she being clever? She can't escape her destiny.*

"Perhaps not." *I know the medallion will give me passage.*

"Whata, whata," he mimics a vintage movie heartthrob, "live without you." And wonders, *arse, if only I hadn't sworn the flag's oath to refrain from sexual contact.*

"These last weeks in Mandalay," I smile, staring at his naked reflection in the window, "have been utopia. Besides even though you are older you're much prettier." Across his buttocks, I deliver a quick slap. "You haven't taken a vow of celibacy? Joined a monastery?" Painfully I recall that Zagh, the reformed comedian, was a psychological prisoner in Burma for five tortured years. *Why isn't he reinventing himself as my lover?*

Zagh smiles wishfully at Lilee. His vow of celibacy no longer holds him with the same intensity it once did. As she speaks, he yearns to kiss her.

"Your body is honey to my mouth," his voice a forced whisper. "I need more time to navigate the Nile of you."

Studying his reflection in the window, I don't believe him but relish his words.

"You are my Cleopatra."

"Didn't think you knew Shakespeare," I say sarcastically to his reflection. "You're Mark Anthony. No. More like Puck or a Midsummer's Night fairy."

"Careful, even we comedians have fragile hearts."

Your beautiful body reminds me of the coming winter of our lives. You're summer, full of beauty and robust. I am still in the spring of my youth. And am blinded by passion. The winter of our mortality awaits both of us. Even in my youth I lust for your seemingly ageless beauty more than your body. Mandalay has an abundance of candy cane men, who would fly to my bed. If I could pluck their sweet youth, I'd stave off my winter. Their pretty bodies don't excite me. Their hot

115

touch is cold. Their honey turns to gritty sugar. Winter will gather these candy cane bodies. Stack them in earthen graves.

"Love me. I love you," like so many times before the words roll off my lips and evaporate. *Does my meaning come from the heart,* I ponder, *or just more vapor?*"

"You're a great heart," he smiles. "And you have great legs."

"Is love," I whisper, turning towards him, "stronger than death?"

"Don't go blooming philosophical on me."

"Tell me one of your political jokes."

"When I search the InterSocial, I scroll to the end, to see the only reliable news. Obituaries." He laughs.

"If I could view the local New Burmese InterSocial, isn't it the truth?" I frown, glaring at my comedian.

"The government re-edits the news," he adds seriously. "More of this and less of that. Only good news is allowed to bubble to the top. The rest is buried.

"Speaking of information, you promised to help locate my father."

"Never promised. Only offered to try. You make it sound like a confounded moral obligation."

"Don't go falling on your blimey British sword to avoid your pledge," I say laying down next to him. "Perhaps we need time apart."

A faint aroma anoints his body. *I remember smelling this sweetness sometimes on Sam.*

Twenty-Six

My Lilee, you are ready to abandon Zagh like you tried with Sam and even attempted with Abba. No respect for discarded lovers. Get over it. There's more grief to come. By the way let's not fall in love with this camera thing.

 In Mandalay, the days slip by quickly as I become more confident with camera techniques. I become an expert at concealing the camera under my loose Ainygi, shooting through a slight opening in front. I maintain a smile to attract attention to my face, diverting eyes away from my camera. I'm intrigued by the different ethnic groups in the streets—the Bamar, Shan, and Kayah. The simple textures in their faces, especially the elderly, express the neglect and poverty they endure.

The menagerie of subjects is addictive to shoot.

Outside a street shop, a tiny woman in a colorful sarong works a loom, creating an intricate pattern in blue, yellow, and red stripes. On another small loom, her companion produces a cotton sarong in spirals and twisted chain designs. In the alley shops, artisans and crafts people work in gold, silver, wood, and ivory. The beauty of blood red lacquer war chests and tables competes with silver bowls and bells. Fathers and sons throw pottery flower pots, cooking pots, and water jars. Shriveled men pound gold leaf into strips between bamboos. A hunched figure carves a boat-shaped, thirteen stringed Burma harp. His companion creates a flute from hollowed out bamboo. In a circle young men whittle different limbs of a marionette.

Young children search through garbage piled in the streets, looking for plastic to be melted into new products. On street corners, Imperial police seem oblivious to the hubbub. A flock of feral parrots streaks yellow and green across the sky. Billowing diesel smoke half-century buses race old patched cars. A long neck Padaung woman and her three children fitted with brass rings around their necks, shuffle by me. Two Chin women with distinctive butterfly facial tattoos march past carrying sugarcane on their backs. Costumed in royal white sarongs three female dancers perform as puppets. Dancing, they kick out their silk trains. The male dance troupe in princely white jackets and head-dresses, court the ladies with their acrobatics. Head shaved monks in their burnt orange robes, beg Credits from peasants and well-to-do passersby.

Rushing about to document the peoplescape, I shoot image after image. Driven to capture each nuance, I twist and turn and point. With this camera, I do not focus because these are living photos which focus later in another computer device which I do not possess. The technology is beyond me. Fortunately the camera needs little light, and I continue to shoot as the evening black haze wraps around the Mandalay streets. With a satisfying tiredness, I return to my loft.

Days turn into weeks, and I am concerned that I've had no word from Zagh. But each new day that I wander the streets with my camera, absorbed in my work, I begin to forget Zagh, as if he were a distant history like Abba and my son.

An evening knock at the door startles Flower and Lover who scatter. Since I don't have friends in Mandalay, I calculate whether to reach for my Glock.

A beige envelope slips under the door. Throwing open the door, I glance up and down the hall. Nobody. Bolting the door and sitting cross-legged on the floor, I puzzle at the envelope with my name written in perfect calligraphy. It appears to be a formal invitation to a wedding. Except for Zagh, I don't know anyone in Mandalay, and he never spoke of close friends.

Slowly removing the embossed announcement, I read: "With deepest condolences, the Imperial city of Mandalay with heartfelt sorrow announces the passing of a true citizen . . ." *Zagh is dead!*

The disbelief turns my belly into a knot. I lean over with the dry heaves. "Comics don't die; they're reborn into a new routine," I shout, trying to console myself with bad jokes. "Zagh's routines were so bad, he didn't make a living. He was already deceased."

The announcement reveals that the three-day funeral celebration begins tomorrow and ends with a special cremation reserved for a celebrity.

During the next two days, I cannot drag myself out of bed. *It is all too great for me to bear.* "He can't be dead. Funny. Full of life," I shout to my tortoiseshell cats who scamper. "If only I was with him, to protect him." *Whom am I kidding? Couldn't harm a sand flea to save Zagh.* In my heart I sense he was killed.

"Arse. I'm stupid, arse." Both cats stare. I struggle to relive some passionate memories of Zagh. *Can't allow them to slip away.* Squeezing the amulet, my lavender mascara runs black.

Early on the third day, I decide to drag myself to the funeral. Slowly I dress in a black sarong, white Aingi, and ebony net shawl. I decide to walk, hoping the fresh air and exercise will defuse my anger.

On the way to the funeral, I stop at the King's Tea Shop where Zagh and I frequently met. With a cup of strong tea, I soothe my grief. I will need courage and fortitude to ask the unanswered questions. My limbs ache, but my resolve is undaunted.

The waiter does not know the details of Zagh's demise. "Very mysterious, Madame, very mysterious. He a well-known comedian, very famous. His body not able to come to city because he died away from home. Burial outside of city at cardboard town," he shakes his head, then scurries to his next customer.

The funeral must be on the outskirts of Mandalay somewhere in shantytown where he first took me to shoot pictures.

The last monarch's Palace looks less royal as I slowly walk past, dreading my destination. The Bougainvillea cascading from the palace walls have lost their sweet smell.

Next, the kaleidoscope of peasants and shops does not have the same fascination as when Zagh and I browsed them together. *Glad I forgot my camera.*

"I miss you, Zagh, even though we were together for such a short time. I didn't really know you, did I?" My low rambling conversation with Zagh brings stares from passersby. *Your death is another reminder of the loss of my son, Abba and even Sam. Every relationship I touch burns. Burns.* Under my Aingi, I clench the amulet.

As I approach shantytown, I see the Buddhist funeral in progress in a no man's land between the desperation of squalor town and the prosperity of Mandalay. Hidden from view, his coffin sets atop a chartreuse and gold decorated scaffolding.

"The fluttering flags ward off evil spirits," in perfect English offers a smiling young monk who recognizes me as an outsider. "Offerings of water, candles, and food are left for his spirit which lingers several days." The monk points to a generous overflowing of gifts mixed with fresh flowers.

"Father, ah, brother, please point out Zagh's family that I may pay my respects."

"As far as anyone knows," the monk carefully remarks, "he has no family, at least in Burma. Quite without fanfare, Zagh appeared in Mandalay and proceeded to become our most popular comedian, a political comic poking fun at the Imperial state. Always on the verge of being silenced; I believe he was indeed imprisoned."

A passing elderly couple I recognize from shantytown shouts "Eight quarters"—the old rebellion rally cry.

"Shush, shush, my good Buddhists," chastises the monk. "We do not want the good Imperial police to interrupt Zagh's rebirth to his next life cycle." The monk shouts prayerfully after the elderly couple, "Good citizens continue on your path to Enlightenment." Turning towards me, the monk whispers, "One cannot be too careful these days."

"Was Zagh Buddhist?"

"In the endless cycle of existence," the monk explains, "it does not matter whether he was or wanted to be a Buddhist. Our faith is that he leaves his body behind to be reborn, again and again until he reaches Nirvana."

"How does one know when he attains Nirvana?"

"One severs himself from his past greed and anger," continues the monk, "and acquires wisdom which consists of many right virtues, among them right action and right mindfulness."

"Personally I have concerns with reincarnation," touching the blue Lotus tattoo under my blouse, "resolving the question of good and evil. I'm more comfortable with a loving God, redeeming me."

"Buddhism has us resolve our pain by ourselves," offers the monk. "Each of our religious beliefs provides insights."

"From what I knew of Zagh, he has a long way to go, many rotations," I counter with some humor to relieve my anguish.

"You grieve much in your culture. Here we do not mourn long. The dead person is simply shedding his body to begin a new cycle."

His theology does not ease my pain; I change the subject. "What are the circumstances of his demise?"

"Rumor has it that he was caught in a military sweep of cardboard town," whispers the monk cautiously.

"Murdered?"

"No one knows for sure. In the great scheme of cycles, there are no accidents."

"Assassinated?" I gingerly entertain the idea, fearful that he was a target of the Coterie.

"He and the Imperial state played roles. Zagh, the rodent, antagonized the political state, the Imperial Tiger. When the tiger thought it was supreme, Zagh nibbled the beast's tail. Yes, sometimes it swatted him, imprisoned him. It was a contest," grins the monk.

"It was a deadly sport for Zagh," I prayerfully offer.

The monk redirects our conversation for the betterment of Zagh's spirit, by holding up a small well-used basket. "By alms and prayers, your good deeds hasten his rebirth to a better life." I offer the few Pya coins acquired in Mandalay.

"I would like to view his body for the last time, but the coffin is placed so high."

"His body is badly burnt. The corpse could not be dressed in his best clothes. Consequently, it is wrapped in a silk shroud."

In disbelief, I close my eyes to imagine what's left of him in the elaborately decorated coffin, with gold tassels and waving mauve silks.

With the dull sound of a bell, the monk breaks the earthen water pot beneath the coffin. The crowd grows silent.

"It is the appointed time," states the monk solemnly. He escorts me through the weeping crowd. We stop at a large wooden pagoda. Decorated in turquoise and red it sits as a mastless, long ship on wooden wheels. Its flat wooden sides are carved with fearful dragons in sun reds and moon yellows. I stare in awe. It's a boat without a sea.

"This celestial chariot will carry the body," my monk respectfully points to the highest nearby hill. Punctuated by loud crying, a group of saffron yellow robed monks lowers the coffin from the scaffolding and slides it into the chariot. These same monks, like beasts of burden, pick up the chariot's yoke, and a slow cortège shuffles to the hilltop. We mourners follow behind the celestial chariot walking to a rhythmic chanting by the monks.

On this day, the descending Black Blizzard curtain brings night sooner as the procession reaches the crest of the hill. The monks religiously remove the coffin from the belly of the chariot and deposit it onto a prepared pyre of fragrant sandalwood. Profanely, the coffin looks like a dark cherry decorating a cupcake of wood. I want to laugh and cry at the same time.

With torches, the monks light the pyre and fireworks. A heavenly fragrance wafts over the mourners, producing more wailing. Skyrockets are incense flying to the darkening sky. "Pop, pop. Pop. Bang, bang. Pop," escorts his spirit.

In a manner of minutes, the coffin and Zagh are completely consumed.

In the dark I stare at the pile of ashes. Reaching for the arm of my monk, to quiet my anxiety, I am shocked to realize that I am alone. The mourners are gone. The outcasts have retreated to shantytown. The monks have departed.

Slowly I turn completely around, hoping to see one human face. None. My gaze is met by the empty celestial chariot, which is now a beached leviathan with its belly cut open. Into the bowels of the beast I stare, desperate to cry.

Still, no tears come.

Twenty-Seven

Pacing Lilee's window ledge again and again I peer into her Mandalay loft. Where's my grief stricken warrior? Has she fallen off the edge?

 Three days following Zagh's funeral, I half awaken from a nightmare. In my vision, every face I observe on the street is wearing the face of Zagh. A death mask. His dark eyes are hollow. Raven hair turned white.

I see the soul of Zagh leaving the body of an elderly passerby. His soul turns into a butterfly, flutters away. Again and again I watch his soul in the form of a butterfly leaving this peasant, this woman, this small child, and even an Imperial policeman.

Why did you desert me, my comedian? We could've made beautiful comedy together well into our old age, feeding each other terrible jokes. I try to make myself laugh, but there's only a hollow rattle in my throat. If only I could tell you one more time how I feel. Press my lips to yours. Seal what our life could have been, with a last kiss.

I force my eyes open to shut out his death. The window-less room is dark and heavy with another moist body. *Not another lover! Zagh how could I abandon you?*

Sitting up on a low bed, I'm lost in confusion. When I touch my breasts they're soaked in sweat. My anxiety rises when I look down to see that I am naked.

Think Lilee, think: *This is not my loft.* That lump beside me. A man? For Yahweh's sake. Hope it's male. Vaguely I remember walking to a local bistro, a respite from the exhaustion of trying to shoot happy faces the entire day.

Hungry. The Bistro. There's life in the Bistro. Laughter. Not necessarily happiness. Ah, the faceless, older gentleman sitting by himself reminds me a little of Zagh. Beautiful hair. Beautiful eyes.

Crowded. No empty tables. I remember asking if I could join him and he nods. So attractive yet I could be his daughter. He didn't ask my name. I didn't ask his. A charming conversation about nothing.

Is this gorgeous man laying next to me another Zagh impersonator?

Stroking my amulet, I roll closer to the naked mound. His arms passionately wrap around the balled sheets. I remember we were both exhausted from too much palm wine. We didn't love. I'm relieved. Have betrayed everyone close to me. I've burned. Scorched them.

Silently I call out to Zagh. *Did you love me?*

Touching my Lotus tattoo I fondle the raised marks. Rising I dress in the darkness. Quietly opening the door, I stumble into a deserted back alley in an unknown part of Mandalay.

Twenty-Eight

Through tearful eyes I, Sparrow condemn you, Zagh. For days all Lilee can do is wander Mandalay remembering, remembering.

 The last time together, Zagh, you inhaled my hair fragrance causing my boyish curves to quiver like moonlight on rippling waters. My delicious laughter tempted your heart. I recall the taste of your lips on the shared wine glass.

Contemplating my tattoo your last question, "Do we all see the same when gazing at a Lotus?"

My heart weeps as I stagger aimlessly.

Sorrow takes me gently by the hand pushing me off a cliff into darkness. Emptiness rushes by. No time to shout.

Will I ever crawl out?

A Primordial voice whispers in my heart, "My love for you will not be shaken."

In my head the cry of a desert Lynx drowns out the voice:

From the murky waters
rises the blue Lotus
unstained, the Lily blooms.

Twenty-Nine

As a sparrow, I could not pluck out another sparrow's eye.
Yet I watch Lilee pass so easily from a naïve lover to a heartless
assassin.

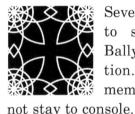 Seven months after Zagh's demise I'm ready to submerge myself in work. Mister Ballyhoo Man delivers a secret communication. "Congrats, you're a full-fledged member of the Coterie task force." He does not stay to console.

My employer directs that I perform preliminary tasks prior to the primary assignment for which I'm being groomed. Zagh's death is the valley through which I passed to become a killer. It seems so simple to transition from shooting pictures to shooting faceless victims. In my grieving state, my prey will not be real. This is my first test and a weapon will be hidden at the site. Although I hesitate to articulate the word "assassin," it is what I will become once my mission is complete.

It's just a job, I muse. *The victim is only an empty earthly vessel, not human.* Struggling against the frigid Burmese mountain air, I pull myself and the unfamiliar rifle to the rooftop railing, perspiring. The view of the modern city tucked in the valley is spectacular. In better times, a lover and I could enjoy the rich tapestry of lights against the quiet twilight. The dark mist hangs later and later over the mountains.

I slump between two pillars. The cold aches my fingers. The pain feels good like a balm for my sorrow. *Time to get this first wacky mission over . . . more important desert rats to fry,* I think tough.

Normally I wouldn't know the who and what of a project, but they determined this knowledge will ease my apprehension. A provincial lord wants the son, the heir apparent, eliminated. The old power anticipates the energetic son taking over before his time. The New Burmese government has a major stake in maintaining the status quo.

Across the short distance, I have an unobstructed view of a sprawling top floor luxury penthouse suite. Even by metropolis standards, the complex is magnificent, crowning the skyscraper like a white opal. Pointing the rifle's scope towards the expansive glass doesn't bring the figures into focus. To control my breath fogging the lens and reduce my anxiety, I practice my slow yoga breathing techniques.

Need to get a clearer view. Methodically adjusting the crosshairs, *I have you now.* My prey is a tall young man in a suit. *No, only a big kid.*

The victim reminds me of somebody. Briefly I close my eyes. When I return to the lens and refocus, *condemnaaaaaation. He's left the room.* Slumping back to the cement portico, I check the grayish sunset and bemoan that my window of opportunity closed.

Cradling my head in my hands contemplating: *my target's a mere child dressed as authority. I don't murder children. Wasn't he a carrot top kid?* I reach for my amulet. *My first failure.*

ted zahrfeld

Desert cats wail in my exploding mind:

From the murky waters
rises the blue Lotus
unstained, the Lily blooms.

Thirty

Lilee never quite acquires an assassin's skills. Her next target doesn't succumb to her charms yet her employer doesn't pressure her. I can poop better on an unsuspecting victim than she can shoot one.

 The cooling Mandalay air swirls me into a trance as I stalk my next victim. Stalking is a pretty strong word as I stand on one foot then the other. The marketplace is filled with noisy bartering and the irresistible smells of Mandalay.

Gripping my Glock under my jacket. *Concentrate girl, concentrate.* Next to a papaya stand is the victim with his family. *Wow, I love papaya.*

Get it together warrior. Focus. The prey is a darkly handsome prince with a plain young woman holding a fussing child.

As I work my way through the jostling crowd I notice the mother is having difficulty restraining the child. *Give the maddening kid away.* Biting my tongue I look down hesitating.

The family is swallowed by the crowd.

Hurrying to the stand I look around and see nothing of my target. To soothe my second failure I purchase a bag of papaya. Heading back to my loft I force my way through the

scurrying shoppers dropping my bag. My papaya, like innocent victims, are squished by the trampling feet.

Shaking my head I hear the cats:

From the murky waters
rises the blue Lotus
unstained, the Lily blooms.

Thirty-One

Like steel rods rubbing in my brain another painful image ignites into an assignment where her role is swapped. If I nose-dived as many times as she bombed I never would have learned to fly. She's a better poet than assassin.

 My employers seem very understanding and recommend that I exploit some type of bait to entice my next victim. *Ah, it will be dangerous, but exciting.* In my breast pocket, the old blood map will be the cheese.

My dark compartment is illuminated by the sparking clickety-clack of the Egyptian Express penetrating the night to the White Desert.

To strengthen my confidence I imagine myself a warrior: with one graceful sweep, I cut the air and a victim's head. My hair I will wash in this enemy's blood. Tongues of imaginary cats will lick my locks clean.

In the middle of the night I awaken clutching the map. My sweat clings like an enemy's fingers.

In the early dawn, the Egyptian Express vanishes back into the darkness; I stand alone, in a whirl of sand.

At the station, my prey is waiting.

"We'll drive a dune buggy to the oasis," he instructs.

I laugh, "Stallions are more reliable."

Ignoring my humor, he continues, "when there, present the map."

The prey moves to kiss my lavender lips.

"Ah, remember why we're here." I turn to the rising desert sun thinking, *Why take advantage of me? Don't you realize you're soon to be dead?* Ignoring his advances, I move to the vehicle with the heat sitting on my breasts like an obese Amazon warrior.

The dune buggy bounces along, driving the grains of sand into every crevice of my fading lavender hair. No landmarks expose the way and we travel in silence. The crests of desert hills repeat as never-ending white waves. I remember an ancient prayer, *Lord uphold your servant. Part the seas. Save me from our enemies.*

The dune buggy battles sand wave upon wave, each angrier than the last. As the dying sun shadows the sea of sand, walls of a crumbling Roman outpost appear—our respite for the night. Before retiring I convince him to stand guard.

I toss and turn late into the night before falling into a fitful sleep only to be awakened by the howling outside. *A desert wild cat?*

The rising moonlight touches my lotus tattoo like gentle fingers slowly moving down my body. I close my eyes and fight my apprehension about the day ahead.

Finally, at dawn, I nudge him. "Let's go."

Deeper into the White Desert I encourage him to drive. "Not much further, handsome."

"How do I know you're not leading me into an ambush?"

"Trust me," I say, pointing to a mountain range rising in the distance. "See the elephant trees. Push on."

We exit the buggy with shovels in hand and I direct him to the base of a large elephant tree nestled at the foot of the rock outcropping.

Digging furiously for only mere moments, he thrusts the shovel into the sand and groans. "This is ludicrous, produce the map."

"There is no map," I tease reaching into my back waist-band for the Glock.

His swift lunge catches me off guard. Before I can grasp my gun I slump to the desert sand.

My prey tightens his grip on my throat. "How fitting. No blood, no mess. Your attempt to kill me is effective," I manage to gurgle before passing out.

Thirty-Two

Flying above the White Desert I observe Lilee, lifeless on the sand and a menacing shadow over her. Is she really dead? What kind of assassin is killed by her own prey?

 Gasping for air I open my eyes to a large silhouette obstructing the sun, shouting "what treasure map was he babbling about when I finished him? You were simply to lure him into the desert and do your job."

Virtually dead I'm hallucinating a colossal piggy in a white dinner jacket lecturing me. "Are you on your way to a formal reception and made a wrong turn into the White Desert?"

"A bit steamy, aren't we? Remember, I'm your Ballyhoo Man who relates your assignments. Until you're able to complete an operation, I'm responsible to clean up your messes."

"Well, I'm pleased you are blocking my suntan. Any water?"

"Be considerate. I saved your sorry purple locks from a desert grave. Besides, purple hair does not enhance your blooming complexion," Uncle laughs throwing a canteen. "Little pallid are we from lack of oxygen?"

Frightened, I reach for my breast pocket to assure the map is safe.

"Never fear when Uncle is close at hand. Your virtue is intact and your profession secured." Taking a deep breath, he points, "Lover boy is laid to rest next to my Jeep over the next dune. But tell me, niece, do you indeed have the blood map?"

"Nope," I lie, "and I surely wouldn't keep it from my favorite uncle."

"Well if you did, and there was a treasure of gold, we could fight the battle, win the pandemic war, fund the antidote with that precious formula from your Abba's trees. Think of the suffering we would relieve."

It would be so easy to trust Uncle. But I remember Father's warnings to always keep it secret and safe.

"Your father called you 'sparrow'—always seeking an opportunity to soar," he sighs, "not to escape but to fight from clever heights. Lilee, Lilee share the map. We can soar together. Make a difference in the fight against the pandemic."

"I don't have a map, Uncle Humpty Dumpty. And I've had it with this assassin profession. I'm just worthless."

"As your father would say, 'God doesn't make rubbish'."

"You're not listening."

"Yes. I understand you, but you don't appreciate your situation. The Coterie will not accept resignations from dishy lavender heads."

"I'll find a way out."

Ignoring her, he circles his throbbing stomach. "I wonder where the closest drive-through is?"

"Never developed this part of the White Desert, Jeune. Belly up to leftovers at my would-be assassin's grave next to your Jeep."

"If you bugger-off calling me Jeune, I'll give you a lift to the nearest eatery."

"You go ahead, *Jeune, Jeunie*, I have my dune buggy. Besides the sight of you sickens me." Then think, *something about this location is somewhat familiar. Perhaps from a dream. Have a hunch the gold treasure is nearby.*

"Suit your rumpy-pumpy self," he shouts, brushing the sand like crumbs from his white dinner jacket while huffing towards his Jeep. "Don't expect Mister Ballyhoo to save you next time," shouting back, "not bleeding likely."

Thirty-Three

My tiny sparrow brain is baking in the sun. Am I impersonating a sparrow watching the present, unable to transform it? Lilee, masquerading as an assassin, is not prepared to accept the truth of what she'll find.

 Watching Uncle disappear over a sand dune, my warrior's instinct reinforces that my search will be fruitful. Carefully unfolding the faded map, I am confused. The images portrayed don't appear within my sight. Not disheartened, I continue to walk. Stopping abruptly I re-orientate the map to the north and a smudge on the map appears to be a sort of shrine. Invigorated I begin to hike briskly. Nothing. Sand and more sand. Soon a shady speck rises in the distance. Sprinting, I see it's a small outcropping. *It's been on the map all along, the remains of an ancient monument.* Trudging forward, out of breath the heat has turned my sweat to steam. Finally I stumble up to the rock formation.

At its foot, I pass out.

In my delirious state the image of a dagger appears, mirage like. The vision of the Magi's dagger is spiritual, like being in the presence of Yahweh.

"No. It can't be," I yell. "the treasure I seek is the jewel promised by the map—the lost gold of the Magi. Father's hybrid research will be financed. The frankincense and myrrh trees saved. Perhaps gold will buy back my Abba's graces."

"I am of no value to your search for the caravan of gold," whispers the blood map. "But I will lead you to the true treasure which is hidden in the dagger."

My next apparition morphs into the ragged fourth Magi carrying "Flower," the tortoiseshell feline wearing a scarab with a dagger. The dagger has a silver blade of blended metals like a samurai sword. The handle is carved from the intertwining roots of myrrh and frankincense trees with ancient symbols. The markings are stained with henna red, like blood.

"An undelivered gift for You my Lord Jesus, foreshadowing death," I hear the fourth Magi proclaim above the howling desert wind. He stumbles. With the dagger, the Magi draws using the last drops of his lifeblood, a blood map. Clutching the dagger to his heart, he slips into the open arms of the sand. The blood map, he secured in the scarab attached to Flower, who springs into the desert shadows crying.

Awakened by the heavy afternoon heat, my body aches from its weight. Attempting to stand, I've sunk partially into a rather small depression I must have dug in my dream state.

Feel something cold. I'm clutching the twisted root handle of the Magi's dagger as described in my vision.

Scratching furiously until out of breath, I find nothing. Shouting through parched lips, "A lost caravan of gold would be of greater value. There must be more to the treasure!"

Looking around for prying desert eyes, I carefully slip the dagger behind me, into my waistband.

The glint of my dune buggy on the ridge catches my eye. *Must have circled back in my search.* Anticipating my prolonged flight to Mandalay I trudge towards the vehicle. Unsure of the meaning of my gift I continually touch the dagger's twisted handle for reassurance during the long bumpy ride to the airport.

Thirty-Four

Teetering back-and-forth on the restaurant canopy I sense mischief in Uncle's words. After Zagh's demise I don't think this warrior can take much more. Nevertheless she'll reveal the secret of the dagger. Or will she?

 "We're halfway up New Burma's Mount Victoria." I look over the stainless steel railing at the sheer drop-off and gasp.

"Your imagination is running wild," says the dumpy hulk in his exquisitely tailored bone white suit.

"Meeting in a tea house in Mandalay, Uncle Jeune, would have been much finer."

"Shush my child," he motions to a waiter. "You can call me Mister. You may call me Mister Ballyhoo Man. But you can't call me Jeune," instructs Uncle once again. "Like my new chapeau? Fit for a King," he adds, tossing an off-white, wide-brimmed fedora onto the seat beside him.

"You drag me halfway between heaven and earth to tell bad jokes." The words *heaven and earth* crash into my mind: *the hot air balloon trip with Zagh. Too many hurtful memories.*

"Two Palm wines, fortified," commands Uncle Ballyhoo to the waiter, "fashion that *heavily* fortified."

"Fortified?"

"Yes, these mountain people concoct a delightful mixture of fruit alcohol and wine. My child, you will need the reinforcement."

"Never been nor will I ever be a child of yours. Do you bring me good news of an achievable assignment which is so magnificent that I need a drink to celebrate?" I manage to blurt without breathing and think, *am busting with joy. I should share the good news of the miracle of the Magi dagger which presses in my back.*

"Indeed, the news I bring is of great importance, especially to you." He elongates his words for effect.

"Should we order dinner to celebrate? You're always hungry. In fact, Uncle Ballyhoo, is it likely that you lost a little weight?" I add sarcastically and think, *even though I don't trust him, he's my uncle. He should share in the dagger's discovery. Maybe he can shed some light on its significance.*

"I'm not hungry," his massive shoulders slump, colossal white angel wings on a devil, "and it's best that we catch the last evening flight back to Mandalay."

"Must we take that rat trap, bailing wired, patched tri-motor? Much rather spend the night on the dilapidated train to Mandalay."

The waiter delivers our palm wines, which are a murky black from the extra fortification. With one swallow Uncle consumes his drink, a thin dark rivulet runs from each corner of his mouth. After a sip, the alcohol is slowly burning my throat, causing me to cough. "What's my great assignment?"

"There's no smashing good way to sweeten the pill." His sober demeanor causes me to sit tall. After a long pause, I see fear in Uncle's face for the first time.

"Your father is dead!"

For several minutes, I sit quietly because my ears surely betray me. "Father is 'dreading' what?"

"Your Abba, my brother, died." Then he reflects, *false-hoods flow easily off my tongue.*

"I don't believe you; you're making another joke in bad taste."

"May Yahweh sever my right hand. It is the truth. Abba is deceased."

"If you lie, I'll cut off your head."

"My brother, your father, is no longer with us. Doctors and medicines cannot bring him back."

Mistress Reality grabs my hand and leads me to the brim of another bottomless pit. I fight this siren of the abyss. I will not face Abba's death. Now the miracle of the dagger and even the loss of potential gold are meaningless. I search for answers in Uncle's face, but he only stares beyond, above, and around me.

"What catastrophe, what sinister act, or unnatural disaster steals my beloved Abba?" Fighting back the tears, I murmur.

"The circumstances are unknown." He fumbles for words. "The InterSocial reports a prominent, well-respected citizen accidentally drowned. His body was not found."

"No corpse? Accident?" My purple mascara begins to puddle, darkly.

"People at the shoreline saw your father fishing and his boat allegedly capsized. The news speculates that his pandemic research is lost. The reports sent shockwaves across Egypt and beyond."

"Where would Father fish in the desert?" My nerves give way to hysterical laughing. "He, on no occasion, told stories of fishing in his youth, in the Americas. He never had a boat lashed to the cabin of his plane."

"His boat washed up on shore."

"Which seashore?"

"His battered dinghy with a few belongings was found on a beach of the Dead Sea," Uncle explains as if reading a police report. "Madame identified his personal effects. No body parts or corpse was discovered."

"Who fishes in the Dead Sea?"

Mister Ballyhoo Man, always ready with the clever retorts, stares at his twitching hands in stone silence.

Futilely I fire question after question.

Abruptly, without a consoling word, Uncle rushes to the exit reasoning. *I play my part well enough. Abba, Coterie, and I successfully faked Abba's death. Now he is truly safe in Tibet as Baba. This poor gullible child does not know she will soon pursue her father as Baba.*

Thirty-Five

Clinging to the rickety raggedy train roof I ride back to Mandalay with Lilee. In her brain the deaths of Zagh and her father are stacked one atop another. Slowly her Queen, Lover, and Warrior die with them.

If there are other passengers, I don't see them. The swaying train beats my thoughts. *Abba, did you think you could walk on water?*

Crosslegged, I imagine sitting and rocking on the shore of the Dead Sea. Gazing at where a little boat might capsize. I pray a big fish will vomit him up at my feet.

Was it really an accident? No remains were uncovered.

Drawing my nails like an assassin's blade over and over my Lotus tattoo until it bleeds.

The desert felines howl in my very soul:

**From the murky waters
rises the blue Lotus
unstained, the Lily blooms.**

Thirty-Six

If only I was born a male sparrow warrior. With my puny wings I punch the air perched on her corrugated prison. Lilee, Lilee are you blinded by your sorrow?

 Back in Mandalay, I cannot bear to return to my loft. Instead, I find the old friendly couple in shantytown and beg a little water and a cardboard shipping container in which to live. The cubicle is so tiny that I cannot lie down.

In my box the sour smell of dead things, long removed, pass through me unnoticed. Being alone in the dark is somehow joyful.

You can kill a man and eat him but you'll choke on his soul, I recall my father boasting. Bringing back his memories becomes more difficult with each hour in my box tomb.

Tears come as rubbing grains of sand in the parched desert of my eyes, building into mountains.

Did you love me Abba? You were too immersed in keeping the family estate above water. Like a King on high, you ignored me. Abba you were a king and a king has many enemies when darkness and ambition collide.

Friends will become enemies in their haste to gather the riches of my Abba's new hybrid plants. They'll tear at his memories and devour him slowly piece by piece.

There is the question in my mind whether he was killed in a plot to steal the frankincense and myrrh formula or his political enemies drove him to take his own life.

One thing I am sure, his enemies may devour his possessions and his business, but they cannot consume his spirit. Abba is too fine a man to be brought down and chewed upon like a predator's kill.

Humbly, shall I lay a trap to capture these jackals? I'll tempt them with morsels of unfathomable treasure whether there is real gold or not.

I rest my head against the cardboard wall and inhale the stale air that fuels my growing anger.

Thirty-Seven

Settling again on my Mandalay window ledge, I treasure its security while listening to Madame's "letter."

 After a week in my box, I return to my Mandalay loft.

Sitting on the bed, fingering Mother's correspondence, Flower and Lover play behind me. Emphatically she writes, "Give up that most dangerous business. Your father is gone. You must understand how necessary marrying his brother Jeune is to the survival of the estate. Return, support us, help save the family plantation and locate the formula." *Though the letter is signed "Madame" it doesn't seem like her hand writing.*

At no point does she mention the death of Abba.

Lover, the aggressor, taunts Flower who is twice her size. Using my chest as a leaping board she vaults at her, knocking my breath from me. Her claws scratch a thin red line across my blue lotus tattoo.

There is no grief in Madame's letter. While death to his enemies will not bring back Abba, I still want revenge. *Their blood will water his hybrids. Their ground bones will fertilize Farafra.*

Since Abba's body was lost at "sea," I do not have the good fortune to preserve his body with his own frankincense-myrrh perfume. Since Madame and Uncle did not honor Abba with a funeral I cannot take solace in the rites of grieving.

His enemies have not eaten his spirit, but they are gnawing at my soul. My flesh aches. Each day I pray that father's enemies will cross my path. To avenge his death I will become the warrior Abba desired.

In my head stop chanting you desert cats:

From the murky waters
rises the blue Lotus
unstained, the Lily blooms.

Thirty-Eight

Consumed with Abba's enemies I, She Sparrow, feel Lilee's archetypal energies in my bones. Her Queen and Lover do not speak while the Warrior grows stronger, bellowing.

 My Warrior lineage is of an ancient race. Tall of stature, beauty is in my movement. A wise opponent will not challenge me. The song of death I whisper to him will terrorize his strength. If you are unfortunate to battle me, do not inhale the fragrance of death in my hair.

Upon my little finger is the imprint of a lost ring, but my pledge to Abba is not lost.

Like a primordial warrior my face, lips, eyes, and hair are painted purple to frighten the enemy. (Really it's only lavender rouge, lip balm, eye shadow and frosted hair.) Lips are always parted as if ready to curse the adversary. My only shield is a Lotus tattoo hidden on my breast.

Death is my weapon. Death to all enemies.

Now I truly am an assassin.

My brain is splitting from the desert feline chorus:

From the murky waters
rises the blue Lotus
unstained, the Lily blooms.

Thirty-Nine

Grief slows the rush of time. Yet events have catapulted her to the status of assassin. Back-and-forth I pace the window ledge. The Magi dagger may be her savior. Or will it?

 Lying on the bamboo floor of my Mandalay loft, I feel the dagger as a wonderful balm under my back. Recalling the aborted assignments to kill the child prince and others, I wonder what went wrong? Holding Father's Glock, I rub the lady carved into the handle. *Need a weapon that's mine and will serve me better.*

"Symbol of you and your death," I scream and throw the Glock. It spins as a dying child's top and lands in the corner. Lover and Flower dart for cover. "How can I use a weapon which meant so much to you Abba? I'll never live up to your skills or your expectations. No longer will I use your Glock."

Who am I deceiving? My dagger will not make me an assassin.

Retrieving the Magi's dagger from my belt back. I slowly turn the small tarnished blade over and over. It casts long shadows on my sparse walls.

Squeezing the darkly twisted root handle, I feel its history. What redness remains in the handle I sense was a foreboding of things to come for the intended recipient, the

Savior Child. The crimson color will be a sign and a warning to my victims.

Examining the faded symbols on the handle I scratch and scratch deep into the roots. I unveil some dull yellow. Bolting upright I furiously dig deeper as a small line of gold is exposed between the ridges.

Hidden in the handle horn is gold identical to the Wise Men's gift to the Savior Child.

Perhaps there was no lost caravan laden with golden treasure, only a small amount of gold in the dagger. Must be careful to whom I show the dagger.

The Magi blade is not only a weapon but much, much more. *Why am I the new guardian of the Magi dagger?*

All night while clenching the dagger I contemplate its message. *The dagger foreshadowed death to the Savior. What will the dagger foretell to me?*

Forty

The Coterie sent her all over kingdom come to practice the fine art of killing. The boring missions are identical, zero dead victims. Oh, I see a familiar man approaching with a birthday card sized envelope and it's not her birthday.

 "Tripoli, Bangkok, or Paris," I don't know and do not care. "These so-called teaching assignments keep coming," I mumble, "as wild beasts to the desert edge to feast. Yes, I haven't killed anyone, but I am improving." *Am I that incompetent?*

The nouveau, gourmet Café is almost empty. With my back protected by a wall adorned with copies of voluptuous Raphael female portraits, I watch consumers scurrying outside like ants before a storm. As he approaches, I stroke the dagger in back, under my black sweater.

Without a word, he sits across from me like we are lovers at a secret rendezvous. *The stench*, my brain recoils, thinking, *garlic, onions and expensive whiskey. How you have metamorphosed, my Ballyhoo Man. Are you suffering the consequences of causing Abba's death?*

The pudgy hulk, in the wrinkled expensive suit, leans closer. Trying not to laugh, I imagine this man is Humpty Dumpty. He falls to the floor, shattering.

"Tea?" he asks in with an air of authority.

I nod.

After all this time my brain still has trouble accepting that my solicitor, my manager, is my uncle. *The Coterie are scorpions. My worthless uncle is their dumpy messenger. I want to break him into thousands of pieces. Abba's blood cries for revenge. How can he sit across from me as if nothing has passed between us?*

"Madame asks about your health." Humpty Dumpty orders pricy bourbon.

I don't respond.

"Your mother is well."

"Madame's well-being is not a concern. Does Jeune sleep well these nights?"

"Madame and I have always had a certain fondness for each other," Uncle lies and thinks, *I have no feelings for Madame but I can't explain this marriage charade in order to protect Abba.* "She needs someone to provide for her and oversee the oasis estate. Your father would have approved."

"I doubt he blessed you bedding my mother." The image of them together unleashes more rage. "Wish you'd become my next victim's so I can smash you."

Ignoring my threats, "Madame and I get along smashingly except on Tuesdays and Thursdays when she turns herself into a ravishing serpent. In her youth she dreamed of joining the circus," he says jokingly then thinks, *can't take this deception much longer. It's killing me.*

"Perchance she will bite your head off one Thursday."

Uncle finally blurts out the truth of his relationship with her mother, "When your father disappeared, Madame vanished too. I really believe she enlisted in something like a circus." He adds, "There was the possibility of real affection between us."

My urge is to punch him, shattering the shell separating us. Instead I rant, "My search for love has cost me dearly. The deaths of Zagh and Abba. Yet you, obese scoundrel, speak of affection so easily as if ordering another drink."

"Obviously you are not grateful for the times I saved your cheeky life. Besides, I fabricated the letter from Madame begging you to return. I want to show she does love you." Then he thinks, *back at the Qasr we could twist certain information out of you.*

"Thanks for nothing. It didn't succeed."

"Well, let's refocus. If you deliver the final marvelously lofty assignment for which all your training, I trust, was not for naught, the Coterie will reward you. The new twist, however: bring him back dead or alive. Preferably *alive*, in order to extract crucial data, also confirm definite facts."

Their method, I think, feeling my stomach tighten, *involves electronic probes and much pain and usually death.*

"If the target is delivered with bloody life," he sounds like a schoolteacher distributing assignments, "and all of or most of his limbs intact, you receive the prize." Humpty clasps his pudgy hands. "Pity you have bungled every assignment to date. It's put me in jeopardy with our employer. But they will pardon us both and provide you the bonus, your son." Uncle ponders, *forgive me Abba I tried to keep you alive by sandbagging the Coterie.*

"The prize!" My heart leaps, *they promise one last assignment in exchange for my son, but they keep sending more jobs.* I fire back, "The murdering cowards. Where are they hiding him?"

Humpty, the hard-boiled egg, pierces me with his peppery eyes. "They know everything, Lilee. They know of his carrot top hair. They even created a current electronic composite you will have access to soon."

My son torn from my nipples; he is alive. Why an electronic composition rather than a current photo?

"But another complication, an 'extremely special mark,' is to be eliminated first. Open on your flight to New

Detroit," Humpty orders, handing over a birthday card sized envelope. Thinking, *thank God they're sending you on a wild goose chase to New Detroit while Baba—really Abba— is in Tibet.*

"Not that you care. They're dispatching me to New Detroit on a special assignment and then a bit of holiday. I will not be around to watch over you, but our paths may cross."

The rotten egg rolls out the door and disappears.

If only I stabbed Humpty Dumpty in the eye. Shattered him into pieces. Who am I deceiving? Haven't killed a soul. Still see my victims as real people who love and are loved. If I don't kill someone soon I'll never see my son. His chapter in my book will close and I stand to become another assassin's assignment.

In the empty café, I sit alone, forming the words over and over. *My son's alive.* I swirl the wine in the half-empty glass. *Instead of murdering someone I could use my assassin's skills to track my son. Better possibilities of locating a fish in a sandstorm.*

Smiling I press the amulet under my sweater. *Mommy is coming.* I coax the last drop of Shiraz from the glass. Concealing the precious envelope next to my dagger, I disappear into the street in search of a cab to the international terminal.

Forty-One

Into the jet's wing I dig my talons watching my feathers fly.
Down below snakes the New Detroit Carnivale parade. Must
assist her in pursuing this "extremely special mark."

 On the transcontinental flight to Michigan, I
examine the contents of the envelope. There
are photos of my ultimate victim who is
described as Baba, *wow*, the Supreme
Commander of the Coterie. His most distinguishing features are a scar on his left cheek and a goatee.
*Without the scar and beard, I've seen this guy before. Why
are they sacrificing their leader, the head guy?*

The instructions are, first, in New Detroit eliminate *an
extremely special mark,* a close associate of Baba. A picture
shows his largeness in an outlandish attire. *Ridiculous. No
one has a code name "Harry the Monster."*

After eliminating Harry instructions will follow where
to locate Baba.

Arriving in New Detroit, at a prestigious island resort
in the middle of the Detroit River, separating the Americas
from Chin-Canada, I have an uneasy feeling I am still being
tested. The assignment package reveals the island is still
known as Belle Isle and was expanded tenfold on a landfill
foundation of plastics and discarded tires. Like the island, I
am given a second of many second chances.

New Detroit is the hub of a mega-resort covering the entire southeastern old Michigan. It's a favorite playground for the prestigious members of society. *This time will not be my holiday like Uncle Jeune's.* I shake my head.

Belle Isle is hosting Carnivale La Mardi Gras, a month long wild celebration prior to the Lenten austerity leading to Easter. Since the Black Blizzard is warming the globe similar hot weather pageants are gaining popularity in northern states.

Sitting alone in a small room adjacent to the main avenue of the Carnivale, I prepare my disguise. Staring out the small window at the lazy mist wrapping its dark tentacles around the festival, my thoughts turn to the instructions. *They are emphatic not to interrogate Harry but to simply kill him.*

I envy these Carnivale people reveling in their freedom to experience pleasure, a sharp contrast to my lonely life.

Sigh. I gawk at the pathetic character in the mirror wearing a crimson, curly wig; a narrow-shouldered, blood red, plaid waistcoat and a crinkled yellow shirt. A large purple, polka dot tie hangs like a tongue. Rummaging through the tubes and jars of makeup, *I hate this.*

Struggling, I take a handful of clown white and smear the greasepaint over my face, working it into every crevice. *Look more like a ghost than an assassin.*

Managing to paint a red, smiling mouth, from cheek to cheek, I stop to listen to the music wafting in from the parade. Tapping my feet to the rhythmic beat, I look down at the bulbous red nose in its box and give it a honk. It is only then I manage a smile and assert this clown will survive without a nose.

Finished—except for three lavender tears which I paint on my left cheek. *Tears for Harry.*

I am the assassin clown.

Fingering the dagger I deposit it into my right waistcoat pocket.

Attempting to take on the persona of a clown, I stand tall, "'Lanky.' I'll call myself 'Lanky'." Entering the crowd on Main Avenue I reel from the rush of wonders and reverberations.

The Sombadrome, the main Carnivale parade, snakes through the streets like a wild dragon snorting music instead of fire. Afro-Brazilian rhythm, a cross between jazz and the old Brazilian samba, creates confectionery sweet melodies. Each gyrating arm of the Sombadrome dragon is a neighborhood of floats, bands, and costumes. Each community or "school" celebrates a heroic pageant theme in swirling harmony and hue. Singing and dancing create a vortex in which the Sombaistas and revelers are indistinguishable. I am sucked into the Xango School of the Sombadrome performers. Euphoria sweeps my body in waves like a lover's touches.

After completing a few somersaults without losing my dagger, I remind myself I have a job to do.

As Lanky, I feel under-costumed compared to the school of Xango, which marches around me, absorbing me. The Xango dress royally in floor-length costumes shimmering with sequins and feathers. Each head is crowned with a massive helmet, blazing with semi-precious gems and five-foot ostrich feathers.

"Are you female or male," I shout, grinning at the closest Xango whose rubbery arms undulate to the beat, "or otherwise?" The question is not heard above the joyful noise.

I have difficulty distinguishing between myself and Lanky, the clown.

Lanky craves to dance without inhibition, but manages only a shuffle. Hiding behind the clown disguise, Lanky whirls and jigs. Fighting Lanky to take back control, I concentrate on finding this associate of Baba.

The intelligence report describes him as a man with a propensity for exceptional dining, rather large, a weakness for exotic white suits, and a fetish for wide-brimmed fedoras. *Pathetic. From the description, there could be hundreds of Harrys celebrating here.*

Looking at the Carnivale map, I see our dragon dance will pass by the Glitz Café, perhaps a clue. I fling my arms to blend with the Xango dancers and join the tango to the prestigious eatery.

My eyes search the crowds for Harry. In the Carnivale, the audience is part of the tapestry. They are costumed from simple shorts and swimsuits to the sublime of fashion. Vintage Ralph Lauren beaded suits mingle with Zac Posen's flowing gowns. Baggy checkered shorts compete with form flattering silhouette dresses. From the report, Harry also has a compulsion for Al Capone fedoras. Unfortunately, I'm assaulted by waves of wide-brimmed hats. The fedoras are like pebbles on the beach, too numerous, distinctive yet indistinguishable. *Unless Harry is wearing a purple gangster suit, he won't stand out in this crowd.*

The Sombadrome dragon of the parade snakes too slow; I am anxious to reach the Café. As Lanky I begin to skip and dance among the glitzy floats while scouring the revelers for a mobster with a floppy brimmed fedora.

Pausing in mid jump, I spy a large zoo float on a sea of metallic cloth, with flowers and vegetation made of bizarre feathers. The menagerie of gnu, ibex, and chimpanzees is not unusual. But the long-horned antelopes and wild mountain goats on the float are naked beautiful men and women, painted in hues of metallic vermillion. The female human animals wear only big smiles and Lanky can't help but grin back.

Who are these masqueraders? The glitz of color, feathers, sequins, and jewelry obscures their identity. *It takes vast Credits to be here,* I theorize, *and rent a lavish costume. Are they financiers, princes of industry, bankers, politicians? Or are they, those want-to-bes? Struggling artists. Musicians. Authors.*

Hurrying past the dizzy array of floats, Somba schools, and Mardi Gras-Brazilian-jazz bands, I reach the front of the Sombadrome parade led by the Carnival King, King Momo. "Momo" was the Greek god of mockery. What the king performs, all his subject revelers must imitate.

I fall in step several paces behind Momo, who is swaying to a hypnotic samba. King Momo is pudgy and squat, not what I imagined. *But he sure can dance.* He's dressed in an exquisitely tailored, big shouldered, double-breasted, seashell white gangster suit. Performing my best somba, I saunter close and stare at the back of this gyrating king. His flappy white hat has disgusting black ostrich plumes. *Floppy white fedora?*

Now beside him, leaning close, I say, "Bang, bang. You'll be dead." And think, *can't very well say "stab, stab."* I poke my finger like a gun and lose it into his fleshy side. But my smile turns to disbelief when the king turns to face me.

"You're Harry?"

Uncle Jeune does a double take at Lanky the clown and continues to somba with more enthusiasm. *What a sad arse I am. The wonky Coterie has turned her on me.*

"Humpty Dumpty," I scream, "Uncle Ballyhoo, you're one of them. You can't be my extremely special mark." *It's absurd, they want me to cut down my solicitor. My contact. My flesh and blood.*

The crashing sounds of the Sombadrome absorb my shouts. Uncle does not respond but reveals a face pock-marked with scars resembling a beating.

"Humpy you've become ugly as the moon." Through my baggy pocket, I press the dagger into Uncle Ballyhoo's massive side. "Keep on dancing, King," I shout. "You and I are going to rumba a little detour to the Glitz Café for a quiet tête-à-tête," I beam a big clown smile, "around the next corner."

Living up to the name, Momo sombas faster and wilder, his white fedora flopping. Lanky is soon straining three strides to each of the King's. Momo is dancing away from the floats and swaying bands. The costumed revelers and I have difficulty wiggling his beat and keeping up with the King. "Slowdown Humpty," I command out of breath. "Racing to your own death? Just want to chitchat."

Just my luck. I will be your first successful kill, sweats Uncle. *Must warn Abba his wacko warrior daughter is on the move.*

His gyrations increase and veer right slicing a wedge through the front row of spectators who attempt to samba as recklessly as the King. The whirling, twirling vintage Dior and LaCroix gowns and dresses, outlandish hats, and velour fedoras envelop the King, separating him from me.

Over the sea of spinning hats, I see Harry's bouncing fedora disappearing. In my futile attempt to wedge my way through the King's entourage, I lose sight of his gyrating fedora. Hopping on tiptoes, I search for the white fedora among the bobbing multi-colored hats.

A faraway flash of white explodes through the spectators. Harry is steamrolling towards the majestic Japanese pagoda and sideshow. I make a valiant effort to push through the masses. Instead, the unconcerned Momo's entourage carries me along. Before breaking away, I swear that my buttocks were felt and pinched several times.

I sprint to the 10-foot bamboo gates of the pagoda. High above the entrance, a curved sign proclaims, "Cloud Gate Dance Theatre, Madame White Snake." This "sideshow" is the modern Peking Opera performing the legend of a beautiful woman and a white snake.

Into the darkened Theatre I slip clutching the dagger in my pocket. Blinking to clear the white makeup melting into my eyes, I observe a small empty theater in the round. "Where are you cowardly hulk of an egg white hiding?" I tiptoe my way down to the second row of seats.

On the round wooden stage an Asian dance troupe performs the opera-ballet. Fascinated, Lanky slinks into a seat, remembering vaguely her Madame's interpretation of the Chinese tale. *Did the Empress Wu change into a white snake or did a snake become a woman?*

In loincloths, seven muscular male dancers leap and tumble over each other. Their diminutive bodies glisten with a hand rubbed patina in the three spotlights. The ballet is performed to the rhythm of a lilting, unseen flute. At times the polished bodies dangle in space, suspended by a single high-pitched note. Mesmerized, the clown in me is jealous of the fluid, snakelike movements. I wish I could share this performance with my mother even though we weren't close. *How absurd,* I laugh to myself, *an assassin clown watching a Chinese opera about a woman in love with a serpent.*

Rising like a blossom from the glossy petals of the weaving male dancers, the Empress appears. The Empress Wu's white gown billows with rows upon rows of silk folds. Her skin resembles porcelain. *It reminds me of Madame's.* Staring closer at her shimmering skin, *it's tattooed in white scales.*

Holograms of vipers and adders begin to glow about her and the dancers.

Slowly raising her long arms, she presents a great white serpent. The albino snake slithers up her left arm, coils five times around her waist, crosses her breasts and its head reigns on the Empress's head, a crown. Gradually at first, then swifter and swifter, whirling and weaving, the Empress dances. The white upon white tattooed skin, silk gown and albino serpent, is a blur of imagination, piercing the dark hologram of pirouetting snakes. The seven male dancers each lift dark-colored cobras and join the frenzied rhythm of the wailing flute. Lanky is hypnotized by the swirling white vortex losing track of her mission.

As abruptly as it began, the music and dancing cease. The Empress and her seven attendants become ancient statues with their limbs frozen in time.

Gracefully the Empress reaches up and grasps the snakehead in her hands, lowering it to her lips. In one powerful bite, she severs the serpent's head, as a child would bite off a candy animal head. The long snake body uncoils and collapses to the stage.

Flashes shroud the stage. Explosions of white light as stars being born in faraway galaxies, blind me.

Instinctively, I spring to my feet, blinking. Actors, Empress. Vanish. A fuzzy silhouette of a man takes shape onstage shouting, "Don't follow. Too dangerous."

"Dumpy," I yell, "Harry, King Momo . . ." Lanky leaps onto the stage, sliding into a pile of cobras while watching the bone-white mobster suit fly off the other end and evaporate into the dark theater.

"Arse . . . I hate snakes," I scream, recalling the evening in the desert when my father shot the Viper. "Are these monsters alive?" Gingerly picking up a particularly long cobra I smile. *These little darlings are tissue paper.*

"Uncle . . . be reasonable. Let's have a cup of tea. Why does our employer want you eliminated?" The pleas echo in the empty theater.

"Would I be addressing Harry, the monster?" I again implore "or Empress, the snake? Or Harry the snake." *Perhaps Uncle is the Empress. Maybe the white snake is both Jeune and the Empress.* My clown's musings are interrupted by the soft clang of a closing gate.

Uncle or whoever has left the theatre. I feel for the security of the dagger in my pocket and rush to the theatre entrance, not knowing what manner of creature I am dealing with now.

Momentarily blinded outside by the sunlight I, Lanky, am engulfed by the sea of revelers and performers once again. I catch a glimpse of the white suit like the crest of a tsunami plowing through the crowd, disappearing into the next sideshow, the Blue Lizard.

Sprinting to the Blue Lizard Theatre I observe it is home to a troupe of contortionists or "benders." Cautiously pushing open the 15-foot glass doors, Lanky smirks: *Contortionists are the only creatures who can make both ends meet.*

I enter into a massive arena, a circus "big top." The clown in me feels at home. Looking around there are no seats or even bleachers. The floor is covered with synthetic green sawdust, which gives the illusion of a cross between grass and plush carpet. Shuffling through the dense sawdust I observe two dots near the dome top descend to become figures on two trapezes.

A crowd of exquisite gowns, dresses, suits, and fedoras gathers around, each face straining to watch the two trapeze performers swing to and fro. Dangling by his arms from one trapeze is a male in green tights; from the other, a female in blue lizard tights. Hypnotically we watch in awe as the aerial acrobats flip in turn and catch each other by various limbs. Somersaulting, the female dives into oblivion and is captured by the male's hands. The green man jumps, spinning into the abyss and is saved at the last second by grabbing her blue foot. Back and forth they fly—two dragonflies mating in the air.

A spotlight, then a drum roll, breaks Blue Tight's rhythm. I sense her concentration of muscle and mind as she dangles from the trapeze. With both legs locked behind her neck she swings into a full butterfly position. At the high point of blue's swing, she catapults herself. Gracefully flipping and darting until she loses momentum hovering in space, she seems doomed to be smashed upon us spectators. As she begins to fall, she unlocks her legs from behind her neck and takes on a diver's horizontal position. Green Tights swings by and catches her left hand.

To thunderous applause, the acrobats are lowered to the sawdust.

All this fantasy is distracting. Through the admiring crowd, I push my way. The clown in me is unsure how to address this petite lady. Without thought, I blurt, "Blue Liz." It is then I notice the remnants of porcelain white on her high cheekbones.

Blue Tights raises her left hand towards me as if to bless. With her right hand, she motions to Green Tights. He leaps to the top of an eight-foot Greek column and imitates a green frog, motionless.

The spectators clap furiously.

Blue Tights turns to me and commands in a fake Russian accent covering an oriental voice, "Madame. Address me Madame. Why you dress like clown?" The lizard lady doesn't smile. "Am intrigued." Madame as a female Moses lifts her arms and the crowd parts. "Come to dressing room." Madame parades to the wild applause and I, Lanky, tramp behind.

I'm like a handmaiden who should be holding the veil train of the Queen mother, thinks Lanky. *Madame seems as sinister as my Madame.*

"Wait in the narthex while I change," Madame orders.

My eyes are overwhelmed by her luxurious suite. Light filters through the intricately stained glass windows lining the narthex. Indefinable mythical creatures depicting creation are etched into the cut glass.

While I wait, I invent a story to tell Madame.

"You come," orders the Russian accent.

Through a narrow hallway, I follow the low pitch voice.

"Where's Ma . . .?" I gasp, taken aback by the miniature museum. Seemingly authentic, full-sized Greek and Roman statues, with smaller ones on pedestals, fill the bright space. Expensive Renaissance oil paintings cover the midnight blue velvet walls. "B-b-beautiful," I stutter.

Among a cluster of mythological animal statues, a lyrical oriental voice like a serpent's tongue, pulls me to it. "You like?"

I gulp.

Every voluptuous curve of Madame's gorgeous, naked body is covered in blue luminous body paint. On a low alabaster pedestal, she performs a handstand, followed by a backbend until she is sitting on her head.

"Nice . . . very nice," stutters the clown in me, hoping my greasepaint hides my blushing. *Awfully familiar in her body, eyes, and sharp tongue.*

"Why you clown?" hisses the blue head crowned with her own blue buttocks. "No fit with Sombadrome parade."

"New tradition," I fabricate. "The festival promoters want to put new life into Sombodroma. Bring in more revelers and of course more profits."

"Clown belongs in circus."

"Madame, you must know everything," I quickly offer, "that occurs inside and outside your realm."

"Perhaps," purrs the blue head, enjoying the compliment.

"I'm to meet my uncle at the parade. Very recognizable—short, pudgy without a neck, masquerading as a gangster in a white double-breasted suit," I take a deep breath. "Do you know him?"

"Divulge more," hisses the blue head, "do you love uncle?"

"Yes, very much," the clown fibs. Feeling uneasy, I grip my dagger. "Believe I spotted him in the pageant. I haven't seen him for quite some time."

"And yet you come to meet him," demands the blue head, stretching her limbs and causing a cobalt ripple of muscles through the contortions.

I don't like the direction the conversation is taking. "We've been apart for some time; I'd like to play catch-up. You know. Reminisce about old times and plan our future."

"You try hurt my Jeune," hisses the contortionist, and she shape-shifts into a blue cobra. "You no good daughter, Lilee," spits the serpent swaying slowly.

Mesmerized by the cobra's red eyes, she strikes twice. Paralyzed, I can't raise my dagger or voice the nastiest of words to my loving mother.

The pain of the snakebite spreads from my left arm then throughout my body. Half conscious, I hear another voice. *Samman?*

Once again you failed, Lilee. Uncle Jeune still roams the streets," sneers Samman.

"Sam? Am I dying?" I choke.

"Fortunately you will survive the venom to serve me and the Coterie." He chuckles shaking his head.

"You've grown into pretty woman," says Madame softly.

My last image before passing out, is of two evils: Sam and Mother, both of whom I attempted to love.

"Explain," Madame commands. "Why are the Coterie trying to kill my new husband? He's serves you well." Then thinks, *can't stand sight of Jeune any more than his brother, my old useless husband. Glad he died.*

"Must I remind you whom you are addressing and the fact I gave you sanctuary from Jeune in the circus." Samman glares back at Madame. "It's simply another test for your cheeky daughter. If she can kill her dumpy uncle, she can assassinate Baba, my father, who is much more powerful. Be grateful she bumbled it, as we thought she would. We learned, however, she has the determination to follow our orders. But in the end she may be eliminated if she doesn't succeed." He reasons, *must be careful this serpent doesn't know Abba is alive and impersonating Baba. Another reason it's time to eradicate Jeune.*

Madame shakes her head thinking, *must protect my only daughter*. Instinctively she thrusts her fangs toward Samman's face, but he effortlessly sidesteps and lands a soft karate punch to her side.

Next morning, I bolt awake to the sound of children's laughter as families explore the carnival sideshows. Leaning against a stucco wall I find myself slumped on the sidewalk. Overhead a sign announces: "Love & Liberty Cream Ice." Rubbing my sore arm, I wish I had ice. Struggling to stand up the shooting pains throughout my body prevent me.

I think I imagined an Empress, contortionist, and a white snake. Also seems I've lost Jeune. If Uncle is really the Coterie's scapegoat perhaps I can confide in him after all. One thing for sure I can't trust Sam. For certain my mother, Madame, is able to change shapes and is dangerous.

"Look, look," squeals a group of children running towards the cream ice parlor, "a real clown."

Standing over me, the youngsters shriek then scatter in all directions. Turning to look at my reflection in the Cream Ice window, I gasp: a grotesque clown face smeared with white, purple, and red makeup looks back.

I'm a failure as a clown.

On a deserted street, sits a clown smaller than life. Her grimy face sinks to her chest . . . not even a good assassin.

Forty-Two

All this flying back-and-forth is exhausting. Half the time don't know where the assassin clown Lilee and I, the homeless sparrow belong. Will she turn hate and even love into weapons?

 Throwing open my Mandalay loft door, I hear my cats talking. "Have you been good, as good at accomplishing nothing as I have?" The black carry-on holding the remnants of my clown disguise falls hard on the tail of Flower who scurries.

"Come, Lover," I motion to the other younger more aggressive cat, as a mother enticing a toddler. Purring strongly, both felines sit motionless, sphinxlike. I crash into a chair, too tired to switch on a light or fill a glass with wine.

"Lover, torture any vermin?" I try to smile, but my dry lips feel like they will shatter. "What have I become? Reduced to conversing with cats."

Grabbing an ivory artifact, I hurl it towards the bullet-proof window. *Fortune, break my bad luck.* The small relic bounces from the window and rolls next to the Glock still in the corner. Lover pounces and paws it.

"No matter what their high commands. My dagger and even Abba's Glock is of no use against the likes of Madame Lady Lizard and mambo Uncle."

"Sam and his Coterie are playing chess with Madame and Humpty and me," I shout to the cats. "Must perform extraordinarily well in this game . . . accept they have my son and carry on with my last assignment, Baba. Yet in spite of everything my solicitor uncle is my target too. *Should our paths cross, could I kill Uncle to ease my son's release? Must convince the Coterie that delivering Baba is enough.*

"Lover, do you enjoy killing mice?" I watch the evening shadows march across the room. "Flower, girl, do you love your prey?"

Purring loudly, the felines recline next to each other, ignoring the questions.

What is love? Spend your whole life searching. My fingers tap out a heartbeat. *I loved Abba now he's dead. Loved Zagh and he died. Loved Sam and he's dead to my trust. I do better in the hate department. Have plenty for my . . . I loathe to use the word Mother. Abhor Uncle.* My drumming gradually evolves into a death beat.

The only person who really cares for me was my Abba. He held me on his lap and told beautiful stories that shaped my views of the world. His love and teachings should have made me a better woman. *Look at whom I've become. A pathetic hit woman.*

I close my eyes and take deep breaths against my growing rage.

Retrieving the Glock I point at an imaginary Madame, *jealous of my love for Abba?* You are the repulsive mother who shifted shapes into the present serpent, the one who glared over me, your child, terrifying me with your sweet, hideous look. Never speaking to my heart. Exiling me to the Academy after the birth of my son. Never did your arms comfort me. Madame. *I didn't steal what you didn't have– Abba's affection. Uncle Ballyhoo, you are just as terrible– vanished, deserted me.*

Hurling the Glock *all this is puffery since my assassin's score is zero. Another assignment bungled.*

After nervously rubbing the Magi dagger, I fondle my amulet. *Mother, Mother it would be so simple to deliver you your last breath, but, you were my womb, my lifeblood. But I could no more eliminate you as I could terminate Father.*

Forty-Three

In shantytown I roost upon the ashes from Zagh's pyre and listen to her laments.

 Late the next evening, squeezing and unsqueezing the Glock in my pocket, I wander through Mandalay. Ending in shantytown, I stagger to the hilltop where Zagh was cremated. The solitude I feel looking over Mandalay's lights holds an empty spirituality that Abba might admire. Sadly, I don't have any remains of Father to bury properly. All I have is Abba's Glock.

Pushing aside what I believe are Zagh's ashes, I dig a shallow grave and lay the Glock in it.

Standing tall on this knoll, a quiet cathedral, I preach a requiem for Abba and Zagh:

"Dearly beloved we are gathered here," I look around, "too late to . . ." Shaking my head, "No. No." Composing myself, "There's a time to live and a time to die. But why this time?" Stopping, I squint at the mountains, invisible in the dark.

"You were my papa and I still call you Abba. How can I replay your life? All the things you did for and with me. You were my first love and maybe my only love. Yet I really didn't know you. Born in the Americas and schooled there.

Not sure how you became a professor. Guess your life is a mystery.

"Now that I think about it, I'm not sure of your love. In the end I disappointed you with a child, schooling, and an awkward profession. Perhaps these frustrations squeezed away your love."

Gaping at the ground, "What good are words when I am unable to prepare your body according to our customs. Washing your hair a final time. Your silver locks falling between my fingers. Pouring water. Rinsing. Cleansing you for the next life. Then honor your remains with aromatic frankincense."

Looking to heaven as if Zagh would appear I continue. "I know even less about you. Comedian. Political comic. As quickly as you came into my life you vanished. Is God punishing me because I attempted to love you as much as papa? My heart is big enough to love you both. My heavenly Abba, you take away my only loves and replace them with hatred. This misery is a fine companion to my profession." Pausing to imagine the far mountain peaks where God might live, "death swallows me whole and spits me out on a new shore as an assassin."

After covering the Glock I scoop a handful of damp earth. Crying into the evening breeze, "Let this earth mix with you both wherever you are and carry you to peace. For I have no rest." Throwing the dark dirt I watch the winds carry it towards the veiled mountains.

In the distance chants the mountain cats:

From the murky waters
rises the blue Lotus
unstained, the Lily blooms

Forty-Four

Shivering on the monastery tile roof I watch my approaching assassin ski to a destiny worse than her death. A person is made up of more than eyes, scars, beards, and flesh. Aren't we defined by the love and hate coursing through our spirits?

 After another month of waiting and mourning, an urgent message delivered to my Mandalay loft precipitates a hasty flight to Nepal. Baba is hiding in the Tibetan monastery, the Temple of the Snow. *No mention is made of Harry the mark.*

After six grueling days cross-country skiing across the Gandaki valley, rivers, and through the villages of Doban, Jagat, and Deng my body wears exhaustion like an inquisitioner's robe. *Flying here on the wings of a vulture would have been more pleasant.*

Dropping my backpack onto the rocky beach I stand at the edge of glacial Birendra Lake, elevation 3500 meters in Samagoan, Nepal at the base of the Himalayas.

I must cross the Larkya La pass by nightfall tomorrow. Toward the snow-covered gorge, I set a grueling pace.

My instructions reveal Baba is now extremely dangerous and is barricaded in an upper monastery room. Also, the report believes Baba has procured the formula to cure the Black Blizzard sickness. If I have to eradicate Baba the formula is to be rescued.

Abba would never share the formula with a scoundrel like Baba.

Finally entering the monastery in the late night is easy; the monks are at prayer. A chanting wafts through the passageways as I edge slowly up the stairs, my sweaty back pressed to the curved wall. Through numerous small frost covered windows, a spring thunderstorm throws long shadows into the hallways.

On the top floor I locate the last cubicle which the Coterie's diagram indicated was the vermin's lair.

This is a spiritual space. Sacred ground. One does not kill in a synagogue, church, mosque. What does it matter? My executions are circuses, but this time I will succeed. My mind bursts under my hood.

Fingering the dagger under my vest, I regret burying Father's Glock. Surprise and catlike swiftness will be my best weapons.

Forcing the ancient door open, I leap like a feline into a cage. A shadowy figure in the far corner scoops papers into a satchel.

A dark monk's robe and hood obscure his identity. In my left hand, the dagger is in a kill position, poised to strike like a cobra. My training is to execute quickly, but instinct whispers a troubling message.

My mind races to review procedures. *Identify the suspect. If he resists then terminate.*

"Baba," I shout with faked authority. The figure does not respond, doesn't turn. I waver between hesitation and action. I wait.

The Tibetan chanting drifts into the room, swirling as incense. The tiny cubicle begins to slowly whirl. To maintain balance, I focus again on the hooded figure.

"Ba-ba," I command. "Baba, are you the one they call the Supreme Leader? He neither moves nor speaks. "Do not resist. You're coming with me."

On the verge of discovery by the monks, I'm forced to act. Twisting him around I throw off the hood. Stepping back, I tighten my grip on the dagger. His presence fills my senses with a familiar odor of herbs.

Confused I shout, "Are you the renegade leader who stirs up the Coterie. AND even stole my father's formula?" Still no response. "If you defy returning I'll kill you."

A flash of lightning illuminates the room and his face.

My mind spins with the chanting now filling the room. The goatee registers first. Then my eyes slide to the scar embedded into his left cheek. His left eye is brilliant. *Indigo.* I stumble back as a child from a fire, afraid to be scarred.

The aroma frankincense now rising from him reminds me of the oasis.

Oh Yahweh. My fingers release the death grip on the dagger.

"Dead. Abba, you're dead." My mind searches for options, "You have Father's blue left eye. Let me see the other . . ." The dark figure opens his mouth, hesitates, and backs further into the corner near a window. A caged animal. "Yet Father wears no scar or beard. Are you Abba?"

The thunderstorm growls outside.

I reach for a small torch attached to the wall and bring it closer to the cornered man. Inspecting my victim, *yes, yes, possibly. But he's too short.* "Father?" *I yearn to embrace him, but he is the contract. Or is he? Are they mistaken?* Hope sings in my heart.

"Abba, Abba why don't you speak? All the reports, Inter-Social, proclaim your death." Shouting as loud as I dare, "Are you my father or the devil? Is this a trick?"

The dark figure attempts to disappear in the shadows. He ponders, *I long to touch her and explain, but the Coterie would kill both of us.*

"We stand on sacred ground." Asserting all my assassin's license, "I have the power to eliminate or spare your life. You have the appearance of my father, but he did not have the honor of a scar. Or a goatee. If you are Abba, you betrayed my love. Everything I hold sacred. Are you now possessed by evil?"

A flash of lightning blinds me momentarily. Bewildered whether to kill or embrace this mysterious figure I hesitate.

When he doesn't answer, I raise my blade, prepared to lunge. At that instant, more lightning followed by a heavy wind through the chamber extinguishes all the torches. When I look up, the dark corner is barren. Baffled, I move to the open window; the frigid air clears my head and I catch the shadow. A parawing, like a falcon, dives into the valley below.

I remember in one of Father's story the sparrow can't outsmart the falcon.

Arse. The eyes, yes, but, the goatee? Scar? My Abba or Prince of Darkness? Appears to be him. My father can't be the target. Killing him I lose Abba. If I don't kill this man, I may never see my son.

The Buddhist chanting ceases and the room is filled with a foul smell like a dead beast. *I've imagined an evil spirit—not my father or Baba.*

Staring out the window, I laugh at the breaking day. A *fallen angel flies from my trap.* Sinking to my knees I fight back tears. Thoughts of love and a newfound hate are battling for possession of my mind. *My love, have you lead a double life as the Angel Abba and the devil Baba?*

My stomach rumbles and I regurgitate my lost courage in the corner. *Why is he running? Running from me? Failed once more. Failed.*

The weak warrior struggles to her feet. The monastery is coming to life. *Ask the monks for sanctuary*, I reflect, then shout into the foul air, "Is there no grace to redeem the sin I almost committed?"

The gracious monks offer bedding in a cold cubicle. Rubbing with icy fingers exposes more veins of gold in the dagger handle and I fall into a restless sleep.

In my dreams, mythical figures of catlike forms huddle on a long ship, adrift with tattered sails. *Must kill the captain to free them.* My dagger's gone; I'll strangle him. On the foredeck, I spot a dark, hooded figure. Lunging, I throw off the hood and see my own face. Gasping, I am pulled over the ship's side by the arms of an octopus gurgling, "Often times we creatures search for bright love in dark places."

Awakened by my screams, I sit up, my sweat glistening.

Forty-Five

How did she find her way from the Tibetan monastery back to Egypt? If they survive the barrage of bullets I'd like to hear more about Lilee's quest and Ballyhoo's new found spirituality.

 "Why the hell are we rendezvousing outside of Cairo in the shadow of the Great Pyramid?" I bellow to Uncle above the roar of the antique motorized trishaw I am driving. "Was that Abba hiding in the monastery?"

"Don't have time to explain. There's a price on my head!" he shouts from the back of the trishaw which barely holds his hulk. "The way you're operating, there's soon to be an outrageous price on your purple locks."

"What did you say?" I scream.

"I said . . ."

Before he could repeat his sentence, bullets cut slits in the flimsy canopy of the trishaw and I hastily glance through at the full moon cresting above the Great Pyramid of Khufu. "Don't understand maneuvering this overrated bicycle. Can't find the gas pedal!"

"Squeeze the throttle on the handlebar. We require more damn speed," says Uncle as a second barrage of bullets tears through the canopy close to his head. "MOVE IT!"

The trishaw tips forward raising its rear wheels abruptly, pushing my nose into the windshield.

"Not the brake. Squash that lever on the blooming other side of the handlebar." The trishaw responds with a loud chug, chugga-chug and we leap ahead like a desert snail.

"At this rate we'll be dead in minutes . . . Still topping 300 pounds my dear chubby Uncle? I'll cut your carcass in big pieces before delivering you."

"This is no time for levity so bugger off; besides, I've been adhering to a stringent diet. You just watch your driving . . . Zigzag back-and-forth to give them a tougher target."

"I'm not a race car driver." Breathing hard, I respond by cutting the handlebars back and forth, bringing the trishaw up on two wheels each time. "Missed the defensive driving course in assassin training. By the way, a diet to you is a small smorgasbord."

"You're a regular lady American Mario Andretti with a death wish," laughs my Ballyhoo Man. "Strictly speaking I consume only five meals a day and it's about time for my next supper."

"Don't care who's chasing us. Whom did I try to kill at the monastery?" Turning my head to glare at Uncle, "was he Abba? Sure smelled like him."

"Lovely Lilee the man is your target. And that's all you need to know." He shifts his weight when a hail of bullets shreds the back of the canopy, causing the trishaw to tip. "Believe they're pursuing you as much as me to make their point. If you don't deliver we're both dead."

"As an assassin I'm supposed to be doing the pursuing," I say. "What if we all just pull into the next Egyptian Taco stand and introduce ourselves and you can belly up for your next feeding."

"Coterie's henchmen are in no mood for talking and, please, I am sensitive about my weight."

"Get your sensitivity wrapped around our situation."

"Seems to me your assassin rating is minus zero."

"Hey, only missed apprehending 'Abba' once . . . besides killing 'stats' are highly overrated."

"Baba. Concentrate on Baba. You are in high pursuit of this villain, the Supreme Commander." Ballyhoo emphasizes, "The Coterie has high standards and you, my beautiful Lilee, do not have a passing grade."

"Played hooky the day the class on the instinct of extermination was held," I grin and then add, "seriously who really is my target victim?"

"Turn this baby buggy of a vehicle around and blast these trackers with your Glock," commands Uncle ignoring my question. "I'm extremely hungry and tired of this desert cat and floppy eared mouse chase."

"Misplaced Abba's Glock," shrugging I lie, remembering that I intentionally buried it.

"What the gobsmack!" Turning red, he blubbers, "You're an assassin; you are allegedly armed to kill. Didn't you read the assassin's manual?"

Motioning to the dagger in the back of my sash, "I'm well armed with my trusty blade."

"And these rascals are dying to stand still while you practice knife tossing." Leaning forward he touches the dagger. "Bloody hell, have you murdered many with your little piece of steel?" Then mumbles, "You probably bartered the blade at some dodgy antique shop after a bender."

"Slayings too numerous to count, like stars in the night sky," I chuckle.

"You're a ruddy comedian and a deprived example of what they're graduating from the Ladies' Academy of Assassins."

"Your Coterie friends are probably after the fabled blood map and not us." *If I tempt Uncle with the map and the story of the Magi dagger maybe he'll tell the truth about whom I confronted in the monastery.*

"Rubbish. They want me dead because I can't motivate you to kill. And my brother tried to convince me he destroyed the map." Uncle shifts his weight and the trishaw bounces twice, groaning. He wonders if he explains everything, would she tell what she knows about the map? He could possibly save his brother by purchasing his life with the gold. *Abba's squirrelly assassin daughter might still kill him!*

Then I think better, *Father would never reveal the map. Nonetheless, should I divulge the Magi dagger with a different tale as to how I found it?* A crazy thought sneaks into my mind and I blurt it out. "Hey, what if the blood map was not a map for the cache of gold but for something much more valuable?"

"What's more valuable than gold? Besides the real map's gone. Annihilated. Isn't it?"

"My Mister Jeune, believe me . . ." I retort as another round of bullets removes what remains of the canopy. "We're in a bit of a bind. You're my bulletproof vest, my solicitor, the man with the plan to save our lives."

The full moon passes behind heavy clouds.

"Give this tricycle all the old girl's got and turn past the Great Sphinx NOW." Uncle points to the serenely sleeping monument immediately to our left. "And don't ever call me Jeune. Sincerely hate being the littlest fledgling."

Squeezing the accelerator trigger hard, the trishaw belches clouds of dark smoke obscuring the visibility of our chasers. Coughing and blindly estimating that our baby buggy racer cleared the Grand Old Sleeping Lady, I wrench the handlebars left and abruptly squeeze the brake, bringing the trishaw up on the front wheel and sliding us behind the Sphinx.

Watching the pursuing sand clouds roll past and the muffled gunshots diminish, Uncle shouts, "Floor, err, squash the gas before they double back."

Saluting, I ask, "Where to Commodore Ballyhoo? We're low on petrol."

"Two smaller pyramids on the right," he gestures. "Target the second smaller one, the pyramid of Queen Hetepheres, mother of Khufu." The trishaw putt-putts towards the pyramids.

Driving through the black night until in the distance, I see the Great Pyramid adorned with multiple strings of white LED lights from its base to its 481-foot top, lighting our way.

"Quickly take cover alongside Mother Hetepheres." Uncle waves his arms as an airport ground controller, "She'll protect us from our pursuers."

Shutting off the laboring, smoking engine I stare at Khufu's Pyramid. It's like an immense Christmas tree on this now silent night. "I should ask for a special gift or just be thankful we're alive."

"The gift of your uncle savior is right behind you," he smiles, touching my arm.

"I'm considering turning over your huge derrière for a bounty."

"I definitely wouldn't go willingly," states Uncle, "and you, my dear Lilee, would have a bit of a stroke dragging me across the desert."

"As I said before, I can always dice you up into bite-sized pieces and roll you in the sand like powdered sugar."

"Blimey, you're beginning to hurt my feelings; I'm a very sensitive gentleman."

"Have I told you recently that I really hate you?"

"Tut, Tut, let your feelings go. That's sand under the pyramids."

"Takes a gigantic pyramid to cover up murdering our Abba to bed your brother's wife." I strain to hear gunshots and think, *I'll trick him into revealing Father's circumstances.*

"I definitely did not terminate your father." Uncle squeezes his huge hulk out of the backseat and stands next to me.

"Madame and you employed an assassin to do your dirty work." I press, ". . . and was that an impersonator you also hired at the monastery?"

"You're not ready for the truth." With a smile he offers, "I've a gift of a bloody marvelous little information."

"The only present I want is your heart in my hand," I reach for my dagger but think better. "You're a member of the Coterie. Aren't you?"

"I was somewhat employed by them, but that's as much as I can say. I beg you to let the subject drop. Just always remember I'm on your side, protecting your pretty behind . . . as well as my heartfelt obligation to find a way out of the pandemic through your father's formula. You are familiar with his work?

"Of course, he often shared the frustrations of his high-bred experimenting." I give him a quizzical look and chuckle. "Blimey you don't understand the formulary." I poke fun at his lack of knowledge with my own British accent.

"Why is that?" Uncle returns my stare.

"The formula is meant to lessen the results of the diseases caused by the pandemic. As far as I know there is no bloody cure for the pandemic itself."

"I know that it doesn't erase the Black Blizzard." Uncle fakes a laugh. "Lovely Princess, if you also have the formulation I have the connections to mass-produce the medicine," says Uncle thinking, *and save your Abba.*

"Didn't we have this conversation before? Abba did not share the final how-to steps with anyone. Back then each of his friends worked on only part of the procedure. The complete prescription, I believe, he memorized and never wrote down." I kick sand on his white wingtips, thinking: *Asinine Uncle, you are the last person my loving Abba would share this formulary.*

Frustrated, Uncle exerts his authority. "Your father confided greatly in me. In point of fact, he believed the world has a God-given mechanism to fight infection such as the Black Blizzard. The patient, earth, could cure itself he hoped with a little human help. He had faith this assistance might come from his work."

"Your answer has the makings of a miracle." I stare at the pyramidical lights that appeared to twinkle and ponder, *what happened to that faith I had as a child?*

"No, I don't believe in miracles. But I'm inclined to agree with my brother," thinking, his *spirituality must be rubbing off on me.* "There is a power beyond us that bestows the earth and all creation with hope." Uncle attempts to bend down and wipe the sand from his stained wingtips, but can't.

"Found religion in your broken egg shells Mister Humpty Dumpty Ballyhoo?" I scoff.

"Traveling through the deserts, protecting you, they whisper that the beauty of each minute grain of sand is unique." *This creation talk will endear me to my cheeky niece, but her lippy abuse is driving me to starvation.*

"It's been a long time since I've heard my Abba's beliefs." I stare beyond the pyramids hoping to conjure up an image of him. "I remember he had a special name for this creative Power."

"Your father honored Him as Yahweh, the identical name he taught you. Yahweh is a loving Father who does not judge and punish us with pandemics. Many times my brother called Him affectionately Abba," proclaims Uncle and thinks, *I'm not sure I believe all this Yahweh stuff that my brother professed, but it could ingratiate Lilee to me.* "Your father was a caring Yahweh to you, his daughter."

"Fondly, I did address my father as Abba," slowly fighting back tears, "but am not convinced he really loved me."

"Your father understood the deep down you and would overlook the assassin you've became." Uncle is beginning to perceive me through his brother's eyes. "Your love story is more important than the tales of the Black Blizzard and the Coterie scoundrels."

"Sometimes I think my affection was only the infatuation of a young daughter."

"Your love was more than just the admiration a daughter has for her father," he insists, "more, much, much more." *And wonders, from what depth is all this coming?*

"Yet I'm not sure he returned my love," my shoulders slump. "Abba disowned me. Drove me away . . . it's so difficult to love him because he probably was instrumental in taking away my son. My *heavenly* Father would not subject me to such pain."

"We don't have a microscope to examine my brother's heart. We are only actors playing upon a stage we miserable humans helped to construct. In the end I believe he did love you. Others played a more significant role in your exile." *If only I could disclose Madame and Samman plotted your birthing conspiracy.*

"Father, if you loved me why didn't you steer me away from the fantasy of an assassin's profession in which I've become entwined?" I shout to the pyramids. "Ought to have aspired to poet laureate of Farafra oasis."

"Lilee, where did you find that source spring to accomplish as much as you have in life if not from the model of your father?" *Why am I building up Abba in her eyes when she must terminate him? If I can't save him I should be improving my status to replace him. It must be the lack of nourishment speaking.*

"Not my forsaking father, no." Poking Uncle hard in the chest, "My wellspring must come from an eternal Spirit."

"And that Spirit of love," Ballyhoo Man smacks my hand returning to search the trishaw, "is Yahweh, working through your father." *Where are these words coming from my brother?*

"Got to be kidding, Old Ballyhoo. In my youth I was a starving child hungry for love," throwing my arms into the air.

"Your earthly father sometimes had difficulty articulating his tenderness for you . . . and speaking of famine, your emaciated uncle is starving." He adds hesitantly, "Abba didn't punish you for a child out of wedlock. Our oasis customs demand that an unwed mother and child be separated." *Wish I could disclose the unreal circumstances of her son, but the Coterie would terminate me.*

"It's a harsh reality to deprive a mother of her offspring. I love my son with my whole heart, even if I never set eyes on him again. The mere idea of him brings me to tears."

"Mother's love is the best expression of the commandment 'to love another as yourself.' You, Lilee give love to the son you have not known without expecting anything in return. You should do the same for your father." *Curses Brother after all these years your beliefs found fertile ground in me.*

In deep silence, I squint at one string of LED lights stretching to the top of the Great Pyramid. *If my father lives I see his future image reflected many times in each light: a withered old man dying of a broken heart because I never forgave him.*

As the dawning sun begins to climb the Great Pyramid, Uncle drags me to the trishaw. "Our first stop in Cairo is a great sushi bar."

"Uncle, stop with all this talk of food you're making me sick." Then looking intently, "If you were me and if by some miracle Abba survived, could you forgive him?" Consumed by his appetite Uncle ignores my dilemma forcing himself into the trishaw.

Forty-Six

I marvel that on her return trip from Egypt she was able to maneuver the flight and customs without becoming an obituary. In baggage I stowed away so as not to be a death notice from a wing flapping heart attack.

 *There has to be ordinary days in the life of a would-be assassin.* I ponder rubbing my amulet in my Mandalay kitchen.

Distracting myself by cooking, *I know their executioners will come for me. It's only a matter of time. My loft is a prison.*

The sautéing vegetables turn as translucent as witches' tits. *It would be more palatable to say vampire lips.* I throw the wok at the floor.

The felines scurry. "Oh, they'll come for me as sure as I'm standing in this mess," I screech but think, *ought to have beaten you Ballyhoo Man in the shadow of the Great Pyramid until you bled the whereabouts of my son and Abba.*

"Yeah, they'll hunt me down like I hunted you down Uncle." From the kitchen to the front room I drag myself shaking my head. *"But they will succeed."*

"Some yoga will calm my nerves." In a downward facing dog pose my toes and hands are forced into the floor. My nose itches. From my nose I force my concentration to my breath. Lover saunters under my arched body slowly dragging her upright tail up my tummy cross my breasts down my nose.

"Oh, arse, that itch multiplied." Dropping to my knees, a broken doll, I roll into a fetal pose and reflect, *there is no shield. My Warrior, Queen, Lover archetypes and even my heavenly Abba have abandoned me.*

Slowly rising I stretch my arms, my fingers, *no lover to hold me.*

Bringing around the dagger from my back sash I scratch its handle harder, exposing more of the gold vein.

Forty-Seven

The next day Lilee is astonished by an intelligence report slipped under her door rather than the knock of her assassin. The instructions dictate an international flight to California, Americas. I, Sparrow, am suspicious of the Coterie continuing to employ her.

 In the White Mountains of eastern California, survives a forest of Bristlecone Pines. These gnarled trees were old when Jesus walked the seashore. During the summer solstice in this sacred Grove, a Shakespearean play is performed annually.

Approaching the Theatre of the Pines I mull over the scant facts of the intelligence report: He's on the run across the globe and then abruptly sojourns to this barren place to review a new play. *Slippery devil, Baba, this Prince of Darkness.* Witnesses last saw him meditating in the grove which hides Methuselah, the oldest Bristlecone.

Shaking my cropped hair, *if I were him I'd change my identity again. Maybe impersonate an actor.* Laughing to myself, *need Uncle here so that I can line up this impersonator and him to kill them both.* Reverently I walk towards the Bristlecone Grove stage, a natural cathedral, seemingly full of hope.

"Are you here for the smashing auditions?" quips a robed stage manager who assesses my black silk safari suit and fading purple hair.

Rearranging my streaked locks, "No, I've already been cast." I smile at the British accent, adding, "Are you playing a Shakespearean aficionado?"

"No. A small part in the last act," says the British voice from under the hood barely hiding a shock of burnt orange wig.

"Have we crossed paths?" I sense something amiss.

"That's a very old line," he laughs. His face is hidden beneath the hood.

"I daresay we haven't, unless you trained at Old Cambridge. The formal rehearsals," he emphasizes, "begin tonight. Have your script?"

"Lost some of the pages in my luggage," I fake and think, *I'll attend tonight's rehearsal and track my prey.*

"Memorize your dialogue?"

"Yes, absolutely," another lie and fibbing seem to be getting easier, "very challenging."

"Ah, definitely enduring," he states, moving closer.

"Thrives on relationships," I smile, unable to take my eyes from the darkness obscuring the face under the hood.

"I believe this will be the first time," he stresses with a lone finger, "anywhere, this lost Shakespearean play will be attempted."

"Lost and now I'm found," I laugh pretending to be familiar with the play.

"Shakespeare modeled it after the biblical Job. As you know the Bard called the play 'Jobalene' because the playwright, in his magnanimous wisdom, re-creates Job as a female, and of course her three bloody comforters, into women. Most peculiar. Difficult to comprehend Jobalene's tragedy."

"Aren't we women more consoling?"

"I gather, sometimes," the hood nods reluctantly.

"More loving," I underscore sharply as with a dagger's blade.

"Be on bloody time tonight. My job is to make sure you play your part exceedingly well," he calls back, disappearing behind the scenery, ignoring my comment.

"Wait. Do you have an actor," I shout, "with two different colored eyes?" Alone on the empty stage projecting, "Would better this Baba never been born. Curses upon that day." Then I wonder about the strange hooded figure. *What is your touch like? I don't even know your name, Mr. Stage Manager.* Shaking my head, *focus, Lilee focus.*

At dusk I return to the open air theater of the Pines, surprised the Black Blizzard has not reached this altitude. Flickering torches on the stage cast grotesque shadows across the Grove of Bristlecone Pines. My imagination conjures demons lurking among these ancient trees. *Perchance the Prince of Darkness holds counsel under the Methuselah tree,* I think, *but see no Baba.*

Sitting in the last row I watch four actors dressed in black against an ebony backdrop. Women I presume, though their sandy blond locks are cut short like boys. Their spotlighted cherub faces float in front of the black scenery.

From my days at the Academy, I vaguely recollect the tragedy was updated to make it more modern. Jobaleen is the CEO of the house of Uz, the pinnacle manufacturer of designer fragrances. Laughing to myself, *very profitable in our epidemic, because everyone is beginning to smell bad.* I identify the most statuesque actress with the gorgeous string of pearls as Jobaleen.

Moving forward a few rows to better hear the dialogue I observe that the Prince is not yet in attendance.

The CEO is in a heated dialogue with her three vice presidents, Eli, Betda, and Zofra.

"Get me the damn financial and marketing research," Jobaleen shouts, clutching her chest. "Has my private clinic called?" She coughs. "With profits going to the netherworld, all I need is them finding a spot on my lung."

"It's just a routine physical," responds the first VP, Eli, in her rather masculine voice.

"Where in hades are the reports?" Jobaleen roars. "Do I have to accomplish all these things myself."

The other two VPs stare at each other in disbelief.

"It's only a market cycle," comments the second VP, Betda, in her squeaky voice. "Don't get your pants in a twist."

"At least get your metaphor straight," the CEO smirks. "I think you mean pantaloons."

The three VPs chuckle politely.

"God, do I deserve this," Jobaleen looks to heaven, "surrounded by idiots. If you weren't my daughters, I'd fire your asses."

"It's a conspiracy," snaps the third VP, Zofra, in her low, militaristic voice. "The Big Guy instigated this. A test of our loyalty."

"Jumping to conclusions," sneers Eli. "You'd have us going to war with the other company divisions."

"The Big Guy," laughs the CEO at the name the three VPs give to the chairman of the perfume conglomerate, Jobaleen's husband. "He isn't smart enough, but I love Mister G."

"Look at the bright side, it's only Monday," states the first VP sarcastically.

"Betda, get the latest damn reports," commands the CEO. The second VP rushes to the end of the stage and returns with several new messages.

"Horrors mother," the second VP hesitates, "I mean Madame CEO. Your son was in a terrible accident and is in surgery."

"My God, What's happening?" asks Jobaleen breathing hard.

The first VP quickly grabs the second message and reads briskly. "That stock you bought last week is worthless, Mother CEO."

The third VP takes the last message and blurts sinisterly, "Your newly built mansion, you really adore, burnt to the ground."

"My God, my God," gasps Jobaleen, "what have I done to deserve all this? Last week I was on top of the world."

The floating head of the CEO moves to the back of the stage, shrouded in shadows. The suspended faces of the three VPs move to stage front, in full spotlight.

Eli is the first to accuse in her macho voice. "Rumor has it, Mother, that you've been sleeping around. Cheating on the Big Guy."

Before Jobaleen can defend herself, Zofra declares, "We all know you've been trying to manipulate the company stock."

"I am innocent," declares Jobaleen. "I would never do anything to hurt the company or Mister G. I love him."

"Your health would be better," says Betda, her timid eyes looking at her mother, "if you took care of yourself. You probably deserve those chest pains."

I scowl at Jobaleen's three daughters and reflect, *this pain I also experienced. There is no greater suffering than the loss of relationships with a son and father. God is punishing me like Jobaleen.*

Sensing I'm watched, I scan the inconsequential audience. Baba is not yet here. Frustrated, I continue to watch the three daughters circle their mother like vultures.

"Madame CEO," accuses Eli, "you sinned against the Big Guy and the House of Uz."

"Show sorrow," begs Betda, "if you repent, your fortune and even health will improve."

"You are guilty Madame CEO of who knows what," condemns Zofra, "and certainly deserve punishment."

"You, flesh of my flesh, bone of my bone," responds Jobaleen, "accuse me of wronging God and man. I swear I have done nothing. No act to warrant condemnation."

"You deny so heartily before God," boasts Zofra. "The sins you are hiding from us must be legion."

"Madame CEO, you smell to high heaven," condemns Eli. "Deliberately you have ground our fragrance company into dust."

"Your wretched health is your just reward," declares an emboldened Betda.

"In my time of tribulation, why do you not comfort me, daughters?" The floating face of Jobaleen moves to front stage. "Even my enemies would express compassion. I have done nothing wrong. I served Mister G and the House Uz well. For all you righteous bitches say against me, I love Mister G. There is a God; He feels my pain. He will not desert me like you daughters. You accuse and without mercy throw me into a bottomless pit. Even God shows compassion for his creatures."

The play draws me into the drama. In a loud voice I stand and address the daughters. "You hard-hearted daughters. You speak with soft tongues that cut like knives. Where's your compassion? Being bad does not lead to misery; just as being good does not lead to happiness."

My speech severs the play.

Stunned, the three VPs look at each other. Jobaleen breaks into applause, "Right on girl."

"Are you here for rehearsal?" Eli retorts. "We usually don't get an audience."

"Sorry, I got carried away," I apologize. "You three were really ganging up on Jobaleen. Seems like God, I mean, Mister G would have more pity on her."

"Thanks, honey," laughs Jobaleen as her floating head and pearls bounce. "You need to control that tongue and watch the action play itself out."

"Have you seen the stage manager?" I blush sitting down.

"He's lurking around in back," says Betda.

Zofra drones, "Jobee, it's your next line."

"I curse the day I was born," declares Jobaleen. "If I knew what fate would hand me . . . Better I possessed a time machine to correct all the actions I am falsely accused of performing. I have faith in Mister G. He will provide."

"Your trust is ill-placed," attacks Eli. "The big guy has not lifted one finger to save you, pitiful wretch."

"You alien. I do not recognize you, daughter. Is this how you comfort your mother?"

"Save your laurels for your husband," spits Eli sarcastically. "He and God have abandoned you."

My God and Mister G are only silent," says the CEO turning to Betda. "Have we heard from Mister G?"

"No, and we don't expect him," Betda states emphatically. "You have built your bed of thorns and now must lie upon it."

"Don't be dramatic, Mom," Zofra fires, "you're a bitch. You deserve what you get. Besides you're confusing God and Mister G. And trust in no God will save you."

"Is that in the dialogue?" asks Eli.

"Just adlibbing," laughs Zofra.

Momentarily forgetting my assignment, I remember Abba discarding me like my old straw doll. *Abba's heart has no room for forgiveness; I am being punished for my sins. Can't fail yet again.* I hurry around backstage to interrogate the manager.

Where would Baba hide? This Shakespearean play has no need for male actors, but it needs a production crew. Between two curtains of scenery I move cautiously thinking, *perhaps I'll encounter the darling stage manager first.*

At the end of the rows of curtains, a flickering exit light outlines a figure tying and loosening theatrical ropes that disappear into the darkness above. *Could be the stage manager or the jackal.* I grasp the dagger in back under my jacket. Moving quietly, I position myself between the prey and the only door.

The exit sign flashes red trails across his face as he looks up.

Tightening my grip on the dagger, I can't distinguish the color of his eyes, but he doesn't appear to be the stage manager. "Are you Baba?" I demand. "The one they call the Supreme Commander? Your fate is sealed if you are him."

Like a trapeze artist, he stretches for the highest point on the disappearing ropes.

"If you budge any more," I show the dagger. "If you breathe without my blessing, I will cut your heart out."

In the blinking light, I move closer and focus on his face. "I will ask you only one more time, before striking. Who are you?"

From the stage, the Shakespearean actresses' voices sound like snakes, and I imagine them hissing and crawling up and around me and my prey.

In the dim light, the color of his eyes are not discernable, only muddy. Yet something is wrong, I feel a fatherly presence.

"Are you the imposter from the Temple of Snows monastery?" I whisper.

He begins to form words then halts.

"Or are you," I throw my words like knives, "my father?"

I feel he longs to speak, but hesitates.

"In my hand," gripping the dagger tightly, "I have the strength to cut you down like a desert bush."

"I am not," he whispers and thinks, *my heart aches, but I cannot reveal myself.*

"Abba. Are you my Abba?" I demand. "The one who nourished me with knowledge and faith. Whom I thought would always love me."

"I could have been your father," he chooses carefully, "a long time ago. But your real Abba is dead."

His voice rings weary, not sounding like father's.

"By 'real' you mean the fictitious father who drowned in the Dead Sea? All fictional."

"You believe your Abba would coward in this sacred forest?"

"I don't know where he is anymore."

"Is he a fugitive?" asks the annoyed voice.

"My father, it seems, became many spiteful things," raising my voice.

"What does he mean to you?" He moves towards me but stops in the shadows.

"He is," reflecting, "or *was* a concerned citizen. He worked to save our people much pain from the pandemic."

"You heap much praise," he challenges. "Such a man could not be real A figment of your mind. No cure for the pandemic's ills exists."

"You distract me with falsehoods. I seek a coward called Baba which means 'Wool' so named because he deceives many."

"Do I look like Baba?"

"Even in the shadows the scar and bad goatee reveal your identity," I point, but can't distinguish his eyes.

"I could be an impersonator," he rolls the thought toward me like a hand grenade.

"You are in the right location and fit the description of my victim."

"Would you take someone's life on a whim? You have no proof of his wrongdoings."

"I don't need further evidence of his existence," moving the dagger into a striking position. "Baba."

"Perhaps I am a ghost," he retreats further into the shadows. "Your father came back to rescue you."

"Save me?"

"From making a mistake," the voice offers. "Killing the wrong man would infuriate the Flags."

"If you know of the Flags you are most likely their leader with a price on your head."

"I understand exactly how the Coterie operates," the voice emphasizes.

"Your knowledge removes any doubts I might have."

"Have you considered some head honcho of the Coterie such as Samman is putting you to the test?"

"Trial? I blurt and think, *would my father be aware of Sam's shenanigans?*

"I may be a friend impersonating Baba to protect him. AND this friend happens to look like your father."

"You don't look anything like my Abba," I lie.

"Even the desert jackal changes his coat in winter to protect himself."

"You are playing with my mind."

"Your father would be most happy if I brought him," the voice is elated, "the good news of his daughter resigning from the Coterie . . ."

"Listen, this chitchat is getting us nowhere. If you say you're not my father fine. I'll kill you anyway and take your carcass back. There is the question of my son."

"Yes, I know about your baby."

"Only a few individuals have intimate knowledge of my son."

"Your Abba poured out his heart to me," murmurs the voice.

"My father threw me out," I say furiously, "did not lift a finger when my child was torn from my breast."

"Do you not think he did," the voice fumbles for words, ". . . what is best for you, to save your life?"

"Enough talk. Come with me or I must do," raising my dagger I hesitate, "what I am commanded."

"The sparrow can fly from the Coterie," the voice escapes upward along the curtain ropes, dissolving into silence.

Looking at where he disappeared, *"He calls me Sparrow, my Abba's words."*

Regaining my wits I realize another failure. *Like Uncle, I will become the hunted. Who will rescue my son from the Coterie?*

A rapid movement from behind shatters my thoughts. Before I can turn, a hand covers my mouth with a cloth. "Breathe deeply," commands the voice in a British accent. "Don't fight."

Collapsing into his arms, *his touch is strong, recognizable,* I think before blacking out.

Forty-Eight

Apologies, apologies it took me longer to fly to the Americas on my own wing power. Not as bad as what Lilee has plunged herself into by failing once again. What have they done to her?

 Awakening from a curiously dreamless trance I try to piece together the night before at the theatre.

Opening my eyes, "My God," I scream, "am blind!"

Struggling to free my arms a warm pressure squeezes them tighter. I can't move any part of my body.

Am the prey to a most fearful assassin who has taken my sight.

Struggling to orient myself, I force my warrior's calmness to roll over my body.

My arms are pinned to my side and I seem to be submerged in some sharp substance. Little pins are jabbing my skin. Then I realize, horror of horrors, *I am buried in sand up to my neck.*

With each attempted movement my body is being swallowed. *Dear God.*

I strain to hear the Shakespearean actresses but to no avail. *Who has taken me to this secluded desert?*

God, I can't breathe. You have delivered me to my enemies. Lifting blind eyes to heaven, *have I sinned against you, Yahweh? Has Satan tossed dice for my soul? I am your humble daughter who fears You, Lord.*

Ha, I see, My Abba renounced me because of my beautiful son. Now, God, you reject me. Can it be for the precious life I brought into this forsaken world?

Again I listen with all my strength, ". . . don't hear anything." Forcing myself to focus, ". . . am a desert Lynx, I do not need eyes to see. I will sense the movement of my predator."

Hallucinating again, *Curse the womb that gave me birth. Mother, am I punished for despising the breasts that nourished me? Madame, you hated me for taking away your beauty. Scorned me for coming between you and my Abba.*

Wanting to cry, but finding my heart dry, I continue on with my inner rant. *Yes, Madame, you taught me bitterness and I was a willing student. Mother, the white serpent, you tried to strike me down, yet your attempt failed. Mother, Mother, I didn't sin against you.*

My unhinged mind imagines the ghost of Madame as an angel. *Intercede mother for me, to God, my true Abba. I am abandoned by all who once loved me.*

Victoriously the night-cooled sand draws the life heat from my limbs.

The only thing left to bargain with is my life, for my life—and that's not worth anything. Yet Lord, is not my flesh and blood precious in your sight? I promise to change, reject the life of an assassin which, you know, I've failed.

Screeching sounds of insects crash into my thoughts. Again I listen and wait. Nothing stirs.

Blessed be your name, Lord. Send true angels, not Madame, to console me. Don't deserve to die in this fashion. I am a warrior. Yahweh, permit me to die in battle with my dagger. With my enemies dead at my feet while my desert cats cry dry tears to comfort them.

Images of gigantic scorpions and long-legged spiders circling, ever closer, fill the small corners of what's left of my mind.

Amusingly, I argue with myself that I am not buried in sand; I am immersed in iridescent soft pearls. *They are warm, caressing.* Longing to be held by Abba, Zagh, or even Sam I drift off repeating their images. *The sands are pearls of incomparable sweetness. I am a Maiden hiding among the jewels.*

Stirred by a gnawing feeling that I am not alone, "You are there my lovely torturer."

I wait.

"Are you the Prince of Darkness, Baba or Abba come back to torture me?" The blackness does not answer my pleas. Instead, the grains of sand react to my words by embracing tighter, depriving me of an already weak breath.

"See I am blind," calling to hidden demons. "I can't recognize you because I'm bound up with beautiful pearls, unable to strike you. Please, please, comfort me with your voice. A bit of water for my parched lips."

My petitions are futile. My exploding brain orders my inquisitor, "Bend your face close to mine, so that I can spit in your eyes. Come, coward, face your captive."

Drawing air into my lungs is minimal now. I lapse into semi-consciousness.

Confusing my heavenly Abba with my earthly Abba, *my son is a gift to carry on your name, creating good in the world, unlike me.* Grasping for air, "I love him. He is my flesh and I am his."

Once again I sense a presence but am too weak to experience joy, fear, or hopefulness.

Forcing out my last words, "strike me dead. Don't play with me. I am a warrior."

A distinctive sidewinding sound slides down the sand in a long S-shaped curve.

Father often described the sound and I know the creature that creates it: the poisonous desert, horned viper with satanic horns and cat-like eyes. In the desert I once observed an Arabian onyx die instantly from its swift bite. And it is slithering towards my face.

Forty-Nine

When Lilee thinks she's dying it's not surprising what crystal-lizes in her mind. Believes she's in heaven talking to me. As if a bumbling assassin could stroll through the holy gates.

 Serenity overcomes my body and I no longer feel the imprint of the Magi dagger in my back.
"So, this is how heaven feels? Weightless and fluffy like a plump sparrow's breast." In the white mist, I see myself gazing at a She Sparrow who stares back.

Whom are you calling fat? I'm a trim sparrow who is shackled to watch again your shenanigans since you were a tyke. And if you think this is heaven in your situation—you've a problem. We're in some corner of your deprived mind.

"Then allow me to die in peace. Have pity on my soon-to-be snake bitten body. Can't you see I'm being squeezed and swallowed by the desert sand?"

It's not a gorgeous sight. Your lavender cropped head is going to pop any second like an overinflated birthday balloon.

"You're a creature with claws. Dig me out."

I'm not accustomed to manual labor, but I'll fly over to reconnoiter your predicament.

"What's that sticky stuff running down my forehead?"

Oops. Sometimes I, Sparrow am easily excited. Nothing to worry about. My diet hasn't been the greatest while trying to make sense of your life.

"I'm hallucinating. Chin-wagging with an emaciated sparrow whom I can't see and her crap is running into my eyes. You are real because your shit is burning my eyeballs."

Au contraire, your imagination is very vivid. But let's not be abusive. My sparrow skin is very thin. Remember your lambasting your own self. Kind of like looking at yourself in the mirror. Then again, if you want to go righteous on me: explain that love affair with your father Abba.

"I didn't have a physical relationship with Abba. It wasn't anything dirty."

Come on girl. Confess to yourself, She Sparrow. Watching your old man prance around the frankincense and myrrh shrubs, catapulted your hormones to jet propelled.

"Wasn't anything sorted. It was tenderness at a very simple beautiful level. How is it that we're able to talk and see each other?"

You're in a traumatic situation. Dying and all that. You reached out and I felt pity. Remember you are blind. If you happen to get your eyesight back before your demise, you will not see me because I'm also your spirit.

"A marvelous spirit you are crapping on me. Is that symbolic? You are nothing but a shitting sparrow in my death nightmare."

Listen, I, Sparrow didn't pick the image of a bird. Remember you were Daddy's sparrow and a make-believe sparrow hiding in the nooks and crannies scaring the Bedouin with your special powers. Pretending to soar to new heights. But a sparrow is rather drab. A Peacock would be my choice to strut my stuff.

"My executioner is torturing me. I'm expiring. And you are discussing bird color schemes!"

Don't get your unmentionables in a traffic jam. Panicking will only squeeze what's left of your life quicker. Besides we need to seriously chat about your professional life on which God will judge you. You're not a very good killer.

"I did my best. Because I never completed an assassin's assignment don't condemn me."

Morals aside, don't you think you'll be judged on your performance? You never destroyed, slew, annihilated, executed, slaughtered, massacred, butchered, cut down, or snuffed out anyone. You're the most incompetent assassin in all of history.

"Now who's being abusive? I didn't aspire to be an assassin. The Coterie forced me. God didn't want me to be an assassin. He called me to . . . I don't know maybe a photojournalist or a poet."

Now you profess to have lost purpose as you are about to die. Let's discuss what once meant so much—the treasure map, gold, your amulet, and dagger. They're all obsessions.

"Yeah, now I realize when I'm dead those things aren't going to do me much good. You, my feathered self, could have warned me."

Here it comes. On your deathbed in your sand hole, you blame your terrible acting on me. Besides would you have believed me?

"Probably not. If I had to do it over do you think that I'd make the same mistakes?"

Well, I had a chance to watch the replay on film and you did the same clumsy dance through life.

"If only my anger and hate could be shed like the skin of that approaching serpent I'd attempt to change this motion picture of my life. I would forgive Abba, Uncle, Sam, and even Madame and beg their mercy."

Is that your only regret?

"My real disappointment is that my precious innocent child will never find me in this unmarked grave. Or know my love."

While you're confessing—what's with this map?

"The blood map is a ruse. There never was a caravan of gold."

Whoa, big Warrior. With my sparrow eyes I read the story of the wise men in the Good Book.

"The Magi didn't need to bring a caravan of gold to symbolize the eternal value of the child Jesus and foretell his death."

In my small brain, a mountain of gold is always better. And the wise men could just have written a note suggesting his impending demise.

"Whether three or four wise men, they were smart to know the danger of transporting a large cache of gold and a fore-shadowing note across the desert. A special dagger was created with gold hidden in the handle to present to the Child."

Lilee you must be sniffing the venom of the horned viper to make up a story like that.

"My tale is even more unbelievable. Yeah, the Magi dagger became the tool of my profession. But more importantly the miniscule gold I discovered in its twisted handle encouraged me to search for the deep value within my twisted self."

You mean even a bumbling assassin has merit to her life?

My worth, I'm beginning to believe as I'm being squeezed to death, is only as good as my relationships of love."

Your past performance in the love department is not award-winning as I, Sparrow have continually observed.

"I confess I have failed in giving and receiving love as many times as there are stars in the desert sky. But I'm darn good at throwing thunderbolts of hate."

Well, let's not beat this love thing to death. We know your track record. Yet can you forgive yourself?

"Guess my God-given Warrior, Queen, and Lover energies are out of balance, especially in the love and hate arena. Perhaps my soul is dead already."

Lilee you are a Lotus flower in the making. You're stuck in a mud tomb. No amount of ego will surge you to the next level of love and a symbiotic existence. Look beyond yourself and me to a higher Spirit.

Somehow I thought I would die in battle listening to glorious trumpets of victory. But now all I hear is myself talking with my spirit in the form a scruffy sparrow. I don't overhear my feline saviors singing and so must rely on my fading memory: from the murky waters rises the blue Lotus, unstained the Lily blooms.

Fifty

Coming back to life is not all it's cracked up to be especially when she's been to a heaven which turns out to be only a conversation with She Sparrow. I can't quite make out where she's impounded except one monstrous machine is attached to her with tentacles.

 Why hasn't the horned viper struck?
My pathetic life history flashes like a shattered motion picture. Stretching, I reach for the accelerating moving picture frames, but can't quite touch them to transform the scenes. Before the film flares into flame, I catch fragments: my Glock explodes. A startled flock of sparrows flies. At my feet is a dead sparrow. Abba and Uncle are filling in an empty grave.

The Python sand is slowly regurgitating what's left of me. Opening my eyes, "I'm born blind, as a baby."

"Patience my lovely patient," says the British voice with comical authority. "We temporarily gutted your sight."

"Are you an angel or a desert alley cat?"

"It is for us to comprehend," the voice laughs, "and you to discover if I have smashing wings."

"Your voice is familiar. Am I addressing God?" My strength is returning.

"Hardly," he laughs again, "unless your barmy god has strange ways about him."

214

"You mean I'm not in heaven. Then you're the court jester," I say, engaging the increasingly familiar voice while calculating my next move. "I vision the celestial kingdom clothed with trees of pearls and Jasmine. Beautiful, virgin boys are . . . "

"You mean virgin maidens," he roars.

"Whatever," attempting to raise my hand and strike at the voice, "as long as they're gorgeous."

"You're still paralyzed," he scoffs. "the drugs will not wear off for several hours."

"Why am I still alive?" Struggling to move my fingers. "Do you plan to kill me?"

"You demand too many answers," he replies harshly. "In time all will be revealed."

"I am a goat brought to slaughter and then reprieved." *A warrior brought to shame. Better, I be dead.* Focusing all my archetypal energies, I imagine my fingers and toes wiggling. Still no movement. Drifting off I have the nagging feeling that the voice is recognizable, almost affectionate.

"Wake," commands the voice. "It is smashing show time."

"Where am I?" I ask, happy to feel tingling in my limbs.

"Somewhere you are scheduled to be, little sparrow."

"Only my father calls me Sparrow," I remark cautiously, fearful of the strangely recognizable voice and hint of a sweet aroma.

"We have knowledge of your every wonky move."

"Kill me quick, or when sight and strength return, you are dead."

"Your threats pose no fear my cheeky assassin. If you do not follow our bidding, we will sacrifice you on your biblical altar."

"The ordeal you put me through has some meaning?" I ask with a hint of fear.

"The purpose," the voice emphasizes, "was to stimulate your sensibilities. Up to this juncture you've mucked up all the missions."

"By almost destroying me mentally and physically?"

"Have you terminated your final task?" the voice demands.

"No, but . . ."

"Need I remind you of your son," taunts the voice. I picture a hooded figure hovering over my son with a dagger.

"Baba's a desert fox. A shadow in the night," I say poetically. "He jumps out a window and flies up ropes."

"In your death dream you mumbled above value. You, yourself, are worthless. Your family and even your uncle want nothing to do with you. The only value you have is what we the Coterie graciously bestow on you. And that significance is only to eliminate Baba. In fact, you don't exist without us."

Fighting back tears in my blind eyes, "I have to be worth something to my family. I'm their blood."

"Neither your father or mother nor uncle love the sight of you. The Coterie is your family. Do what is required of membership in our family—your final assignment. And we will love you forever," says the voice with compassion. "Failing is normally not forgivable. Take heed of the consequences of another yet smarmy blunder."

Lilee in an unmarked grave, in an unknown land, I envision nervously, *and worse yet never laying eyes on my son. Think positively, I will belong to a family even if it's the dysfunctional Coterie.*

"The trial you endured is to emphasize the magnitude of your mission," states the voice with great authority. "You were tested and punished for your sins, your failures. Your cleansing makes you stronger, more shrewd."

"More cunning to tear your heart out."

"Your body, my lovely Lilee, was not buried in the desert. Vipers and demons did not circle ready to kiss you with death. Simply drugged, a virtual machine caressed your body, with electronic tentacles, and created your illusion of being buried in the sand. Our family is very creative."

With all my strength, but failing to move a single muscle, "Demon. May your mother vomit upon your grave," I shout angrily.

"Your imagination was more vivid than most," the voice smiles. "Your vipers were no ordinary snakes, they were dangerous horned vipers. Your reptiles were spiny tailed lizards with the sharpest claws. Induced trauma is more real than actual life. Visualize this: our gobsmacked virtual machine can create all variations of pain including childbirth."

"Imagine how my sharp claws will carve out your heart," I threaten.

"Don't waste your beautiful anger on me," the voice counsels. "Use your new found strength to capture or kill your victim."

"Let my new family of Coterie do its own devious work," I demand.

"Our pristine image cannot be soiled. The InterSocial loves us. People see us as pure of heart. Murder is too dangerous for us."

"Baba, our Supreme Commander, could he somehow be my father?" I rant. "Was my Abba leading a double life? Was that him in the monastery and the Bristlecone theater?"

"This is of no concern to you other than to do the bidding of your newfound family which fancies you very much. And will always take care of you."

If this devil is my father, struggling to put the two images together I think, *he has the formula, the cure*. "The Coterie would be well praised for all the peoples they save."

I hesitate, ". . . if he gives up his secrets that would redeem him. Correct?"

"Dearie these are the manky straight facts. We are not in the business of being saviors of the masses or anyone who defies us; the more individuals who die, the less there are to control. The remainder are beholding to us for our synthetic food.

"If I convince this person to divulge the exact components of the cure and processes for the perfume," I push, "will you make an exception and allow him to live?" Then think, *Father would never willingly tell these details to anyone, especially Baba.*

"Bloody well remember the price payable for your son. Primarily you are to convey Baba to us alive in order to probe his mind satisfactorily. Our machines will have him hallucinating that he's giving birth to a goat then he will reveal all the true pharmaceutical details," he smirks.

"This devil may not come willingly." I gulp and consider, *these Coterie are more sinister than I could ever imagine.*

"To our intense scrutiny, we would like to determine the reliability of the pandemic and fragrance formulas. If he will not cooperate, kill him."

"If I can extract," I reason, "only the perfume portion of the formula it will be worthwhile to spare him." Then reflect, *must save this person on the chance he's Abba.*

The exquisite fragrance would be jolly well profitable for our cause, but it is not sufficient to trade for the victim."

"Then Baba and my Abba are really one and the same?" I propose.

"In the history that the Coterie is forging," ignoring my question the voice rises eloquently, "one minor battle or individual doesn't matter. In a thousand years only our triumphs will be celebrated."

"If my father is Baba . . ." I fight the thought of profound goodness and tremendous evil in one person, *no matter what you committed, I love you, Abba.*

"Regardless of the cunning masks Baba chooses to wear to deceive you, he is our and now your enemy. Also, he is the adversary preventing your son's return."

"You order me to possibly kill flesh of my flesh, the very father who taught me to love God and all of creation."

"Speaking of God," the voice adds jokingly, "the Rabbi asks little Sparrow 'what are you drawing?' She answers, 'a picture of Yahweh.' The Rabbi is perturbed, 'No one knows what God looks like.' 'We will when I finish my drawing.'"

"Zagh," I gasp, "my comedian."

"Da, da-da. Bloody bingo," the voice laughs hysterically, "even sightless, you're a cheeky audience to play to."

"My deceased comic wouldn't torture me."

"Nothing personal darling," he states matter-of-factly. "I'm a bloody marvelous Coterie, performing my protocol. Guaranteeing you do yours. Besides, my dear, your performance does not meet our high standards. You are an ache in the derrière."

"Hell, I went to your funeral, your cremation."

"An illusion," he sighs nonchalantly, "staged for your benefit. You were getting too close."

"Then you do care for me." The silence is heavy; it could cut with a dagger. My heart tries to reconcile the pain. I attempt to raise myself but a warm sensation spreads through my left shoulder.

Another hypnotic drug is being injected. "When you awaken, you will be on an international flight to Qatar, which our spies tracked as Baba's next destination. You will not remember this ordeal. When the plane begins to descend, you will wake refreshed. Your only desire will be to accomplish your assignment with great joy." *Tis a shame in another time and another place we might have been real*

219

lovers. But then again you, my cheeky warrior and I, a Coterie Lieutenant, have our parts to play.

Passing out I visualize the face of my former friend and lover, Zagh, the one with an easy smile and comical personality, has mutated. His face is now a leaden mask exuding malicious smell.

Everything I touch turns into arse . . .

At the end of my dream, my ghostly father sniffs a bouquet. The black roses are limp. *There's more likelihood of the Black Blizzard blowing away than my rescuing this person.*

Fifty-One

Cramped in the baggage compartment I hear Lilee showing off her father's geography lesson about Qatar instead of planning the demise or liberation of her victim. (Fascinating Qatar, surrounded by ocean, enjoys no lakes, or rivers, or drinkable water.)

 My cabin window view is filled with the tiny country of Qatar. *It's a maiden's finger jutting into the Gulf.*

As the transnational jetliner descends slowly over the Persian Gulf I'm invigorated to open the packet curiously marked "for Lilee's eyes only" and read:

"Baba was observed between the Russian circus and a falcon ranch, Al Rayyan. While pursuing falconry he is investigating various disguises at the circus to enhance his exodus." The balance of the report is statistics and a clinical how to dispose of the corpse if necessary. I shudder and brace for a touchdown.

The flight lands in New Khor Al-Udeid, the New Inland Sea resort metropolis. The shores of the twelve-mile Canal Lake separate the coral cliffs of Saudi Arabia and the bone white dunes of Qatar.

For some confidence, I touch the Magi dagger under my black linen jacket.

Outside the terminal, breathing in the pristine Gulf air, the arid heat engulfs me. Shading my eyes I've forgotten the happiness of sunshine. The Gulf waters, so far, save Qatar from the grasp of the Black Blizzard.

The airport bustles with tourists eager to celebrate the month-long, Summer Festival. "The festivities," I remind myself, "will cover up the death snare I will set to capture my final victim." *Can't concern myself whether he is Baba or God forbid Abba.* Turning away from the scorching sun, I do not want to consider the consequences.

While I wait for a taxi I review the stats from the report: Qatar. Sovereign, Arabic, about one million population, mostly expatriates who came to work in the oil industry. No taxes. Soccer is their favorite sport, hosted the World Cup back in 2037, *that's nineteen years ago.* More billionaires per capita. Waving my arms, *I identify more with the poor Bedouin.* These desert dwellers still graze their herds of goats and camels and live in tents woven from their black goats. The same nomads work for my father at the Farafra oasis.

A silver stretch Mercedes taxi glides to a stop. "Do you speak English?" I ask, not wanting to betray my tourist cover.

"Oui," comes a delightful French voice from the meticulous interior. "Sorry, yes," continues the driver with a whimsical smile, "recent expatriate."

Adjusting to the cab's luxurious interior, I sink into the butter soft leather and scoff at the antique pillar vases with their silk sunflowers. "Nice beret," I say, looking at the stylishly trimmed back of his head. "Enough room for a party back here," I announce wanting to sound touristy.

"Oui," he laughs again in his thick French. "When is the best time to catch the circus?" I bubble.

"The Russian circus?" he asks.

"Oui," I reply in a most flirtatious voice. "The Russian circus performs 24/7."

What would it be like to have a drink with him later? I wonder. *Lilee you're so easily distracted.*

"The falcon ranch at Al Rayyan, can you drive there? I'm meeting a friend," I fib.

"Yes, absolutely," he says. "Falconry is a tradition in Qatar, over 3000 years. Fathers train their sons; their sons train their sons. It teaches bravery and patience. A falcon is a symbol of courage. Sorry for the short course in history. I admire the art of falconry."

The song sparrow in me thinks, *Father once called me falcon but never taught me to be a hunter.*

As the beastly Mercedes crashes through winding sand covered roads, the young Frenchman continues, "The hunting journey, Meqnas, is a slow training. It requires much human love and understanding between man and bird . . ." His voice lulls me into a restless trance as I luxuriate in the womb of the speeding Mercedes. I imagine Father, dressed in a white garment, a magnificent falcon perched on his white leather glove. As he removes the falcon's hood, I see my face on the bird.

I, the sparrow, can become a falcon.

The falcon ranch is a sprawling complex of sun-bleached modern buildings, a Grand Hotel, miles of white fences, and goat hair tents. Avoiding the driver's eyes, I pay him, "Be so kind as to return for me in three hours."

"Oui," smiles the Frenchman. The Mercedes disappears in a whirl of sand.

With the summer heat hanging heavily on my shoulders, I am approached by a Bedouin on a camel. "Lady please," says the tall nomad in pristine English. His hair is covered with the traditional Gutra, a white headscarf, but he wears a khaki safari suit. He motions towards the gleaming sun yellow reception pavilion ablaze with multi-colored national flags and banners. Sweating, I chide myself for wearing the black silk suit, Uncle Ballyhoo's gift.

The manager, Sheik Hammad Al Rayyan, greets me, "peace be upon you."

"And peace with you." From my packet I offer a letter of introduction forged by the Coterie.

"I have business with a gentleman called Baba who may employ many different names. He proudly sports a scar on his left cheek and a goatee."

At first the Sheik is reluctant to discuss one of his private guests.

"It is imperative that I meet with him quickly to conclude our transaction," I plead with my best eyelash flirtations.

"Yes, yes Allah be praised. I do remember the gentleman described. Most nervous. Two days ago he moved back to the city."

Thanking the Sheik profusely I added "since I've come a long distance might I try my hand at falconry?"

At first he seems indifferent to my request to engage in the sport of falconry which is unusual for a woman. Instead he explains that the falcon center is combined with an Arabian horse stud farm. While falcons learn their Megnas, hunting journeys, the Arabian horses, housed in luxurious quarters, are soothed by watching them fly.

"An imaginative arrangement fashioned by your good graces," I flatter.

"Exercise and training is not sufficient," smiles the Sheik. "To win requires patience and heart, and a good eye."

Reluctantly he finally succumbs to my repeated requests. "First I will procure you more appropriate attire," announces the Sheik, with a sparkle in his eyes. "my personal Jeep will chase the falcon."

"Let's test the sparks of fire in your personal Arabians," I form the words carefully with lavender lips, looking him straight in the eye.

Into the desert, on a rolling gallop, two matched ebony Arabians carry the Sheik and me, the would-be falconer, now clad in baggy khakis. On Hammad's leather glove, embellished with rubies and emeralds, an enormous falcon is perched, wearing a white leather hood with matching jewels. After several miles, Hammad raises his free hand and the Arabians stop. The desert terrain is barren except for the sand winds, which are beginning to moan.

"The desert devils will bring the northern winds," called, Shamel. He leans closer, "Very soon, a blinding sandstorm."

"Have we time," I can't help admiring his finely chiseled, handsome face, "to hunt?"

"Yes, Lady Lilee. We hunt the bird called 'houbara bustard' which migrates through the desert."

"Did you say 'bastard'?" I try to hear above the rising winds.

"No, Ms. Lilee, bustard," laughs the sheik. "Big bird like Heron, very fast, delicious meat." Following his signal, the falcon flaps its great wings, shoots to the sky, and vanishes.

After waiting in silence about half an hour, "How do you track him?" I ask, growing nervous over the impending sandstorm.

"*She* . . . falcon is a she. Very fast. Locates prey. Kills."

"How long? I don't trust this weather."

"Soon," Hammad leans even closer. "You help falcon. Think as falcon. Become one with the huntress."

He gives me a look that pierces; he is serious. My attempts to focus are waylaid by a quick thought: *Sheik is the falcon and I am the sparrow.*

"You have intended? Husband?"

"Yes. Yes." I wish that I had the power to blush. It would be advantageous.

The Sheik is noticeably disappointed and bellows in an ancient tongue. In the darkening sky appears a shadowy speck and, as if by sorcery, the falcon lands on his glove. "Hunting too late in season," the Sheik frowns. "Devil sandstorm approaching soon."

Deep in my gut, I feel the disappointment of the unfulfilled hunt. I anticipated the thrill of a kill.

Now I sense the loss of honor. The Sheik and my Abba are both probably disappointed because I'm a failure as a falconer.

As our Arabian stallions outrace the sandstorm, the Mercedes awaits me like another beast of prey. Anxious to escape, I offer my hand to the Sheik who holds it tightly, "Husband? Intended?"

Breaking free, "yes, very strong and jealous," I shout sliding into the Mercedes' belly. "Qatar International Hotel, quickly please." Shaking the desert sand from my purple cropped hair, I lightly finger the amulet. My other hand finds the dagger. *If I am to succeed as an assassin I need to kill two birds with one big stone. First I, the timid sparrow, must die to become the mighty falcon. Then second, eliminate my victim. Or save him, whomever he is.* Leaning back I reflect, *when I retire after this last mission I'll raise frankincense and myrrh trees as nests for the desert sparrows and write poetry. Countless, countless poems celebrating my high adventures.* I laugh aloud, but my Mister French chauffeur does not notice.

Fifty-Two

Wow, I'm blinded by the multicolored display of spotlights electrifying the night as I grasp the striped canvas pavilion. Another circus? Lilee's life turns into a sideshow.

 The next day I am once again a child, absorbing the anticipation and smells of the circus. This is no ordinary three-ring Barnum & Bailey Circus. High above the main rings, the electronic banner in three-story letters spells out Cirque du Grati, *Circus of the Great.* The mega circus is seven gigantic rings, multiple galleries, open-air salons, and cafés as far as I can see disappearing over the electrified horizon.

A gaggle of clattering clowns requires three days to perform their antics across seven magical stages.

My body pulsates with bizarre music. The seat is programmed to vibrate to the symphonic electronic melodies.

Exotic animals dyed in rainbow colors perform super-human feats to the rhythms. In harmony, aerialists fly on invisible wings among perches floating high in the pavilions. Gorgeous Russian women over nine feet tall, parade in translucent gowns, decorated with diamonds and rubies. Male acrobats more beautiful than their female counterparts whirl and jump in unison as gazelles. A ballet of acrobats, contortionists, and fierce beasts intertwine in a choreographed chaos.

In this circus extraordinaire, lounging in a luxurious seat, my mind envisions Father seated on the bench next to me in a little three-ring circus in Cairo. The performers, I don't remember, only the excitement of the crowd and my genuine happiness as Abba squeezes my hand.

Today the old circus has transformed into the new Cirque—unlike my life, I think as the mile-wide Cirque rings begin to move. The menagerie of albino giraffes, psychedelically painted elephants, massively horned gnus, sequined-dressed ibex, and yaks with exaggerated crimson haircuts parade on a stage rotating left. Then, slowly coming into view and stopping in front is the stage ring from the right.

A composite of Renaissance city and Caribbean island takes shape before my eyes. Florentine du St. Costra materializes, promising every appetite and curiosity that passions can imagine.

Resplendent men and handsome women in vintage Victorian costumes sparkling with jewelry, lace, and exaggerated hats, stroll across a 15th century Palazzo. One hundred forty-eight Greek statues cast a multitude of colors across a palatial Riverside French café. Gigantic women with champagne skin wearing blood red ballroom gowns sip wine from five-foot goblets, while flirting with well-decorated generals, their long pencil mustaches resting on their epaulets.

Bejeweled bikini-clad Amazon women and sublime, tall boys slide on waterfalls which begin high in the deep blue pavilion sky and end in pink foaming fountains.

A lagoon overflowing with silver coins spilling onto a black sand beach sprawls sensually at the foot of a 27-story volcano. Plumes of purple smoke erupt to a Brazilian beat of blues, soul, and jazz.

A mariachi band consisting of New Orleans trombones and horns moves shoulder to shoulder with violins and cellos in tuxes, flanked by Buddhists playing singing bowls, and led by African drummers, float across the sky.

Among the absurd and beautiful pageantry struts a horde of Gypsy jugglers, contortionist, and mimes. Fascinated by their sleek, silver painted bodies wearing belts of hammered gold, I admire their graceful, poetic agility. Like alien creatures, they glide with precision, not missing a beat. If only I had pen and paper to capture the mysterious beauty in words.

Aromas of synthetic cotton candy, foreign smoked meats, perfumed circus performers, sweaty elephants, camels, and giraffes blend into a pungent mist. The combined fragrance is visibly alive, dancing in the multicolored spotlights. It lifts as incense to the heavens, captured by the thirty-five story high tent top.

My eyes burn from the sweetness.

The music, smell, and color wrap me into a false security. Surveying the audience for Baba I observe a young mother holding a bare bellied, well-behaved baby. The child reminds me of mine. Closing my eyes, I squeeze the golden amulet which grows warmer with my son's lock of hair. Abruptly I push the medallion away.

Why not give up this chase for Baba and my son? I could hide away in the circus. Live in this never, never land as a clown.

Fifty-Three

As I settle in a miniature cherry tree I wonder how she will locate Baba in this vast Cirque. There seems to be familiar faces observing her. Now I remember the sounds of glass shards calling like death.

 On my second day at the Cirque du Grati midway, I hurry through groves of miniature cherry trees.

Standing at the concierge desk, I peer into the 25-foot long desktop which appears to be a deep pool of shimmering water. When I prop my right elbow on the surface, it becomes a solid desktop. Leaning closer, an Asian cupid doll with a cracked porcelain face in a pink kimono scans my pendant. She reminds me of Madame in another disguise, *they have sent her to spy on me. The whole world has gone mad.*

Turning to observe who else is watching I drop my left hand, which passes through the solid surface of the desktop.

"Whoa, ouch, ouch," I scream and then laugh when I pull out a large iridescent Koi sucking my thumb. The kimono concierge speaks harshly to the flopping fish while giggling serpent-like. She strokes the Koi which releases my thumb, rolls over on its tummy and disappears into the desktop. Pink Kimono glares and gestures for me to breathe deeply. Taking in several cavernous breaths, I feel calm and ponder, *usually sweet fragrance.*

During the short span of my "fishing expedition," the cherry trees blossomed a crimson pink and dropped their petals.

My warm remembrance of fragrances from Father's favorite olive and frankincense trees at the Farafra oasis is interrupted by heavy shuffling feet. Two burly sumos bow politely and escort me across the cherry tree knoll into the managing director's office.

Director Sam, as his brass desk plate indicates, is a tall Chinese with a tarnished crew cut. Sam reminds me of an elderly Samman who aged prematurely like the dying cherry blossoms outside. *Am I getting paranoid? Or is the whole cast of Coterie characters here scrutinizing?*

As I present another letter of introduction, each muscular hand rotates three golden meditation balls. *Click, click, click. Click, click, click.*

"Yes, okay, sure," repeats the crew cut with a slight British accent, "whom do you seek?"

Without divulging my true purpose I briefly describe Baba.

"*Click,* sure. *Click,* okay. *Click,* yes," the crew cut nods. "Must have grave consequences if you seek this creature so diligently."

The two burly sumos reappear at my side and gently escort me back through the spent cherry blossom groves and deposit me in front of a dilapidated storefront. Bowing politely, they fade into the lingering blossom fragrance.

Sweet Jesus, cautiously forms on my breath. *What are the chances of Baba being served up right here? It's too easy.*

I read the dangling sign over the entrance: "House of Images." Gripping the dagger under my suit jacket, I cautiously push past the faded scarlet door.

A pungent smell closes in on me. As my eyes adjust to the diffused light, I see what appear to be large pieces of broken mirrors standing randomly scattered throughout the room.

Tightening my grip on the dagger, I approach the nearest ten-foot triangular mirror and examine the dirty glass. I see nothing, not even a reflection.

Then, as if a stage curtain rises in the mirror, I as a teenager chase a boy among fallen Roman grave markers. Leaping back the scene evolves into a young Commandant Sam pursuing me. Turning quickly, I try to locate the digital projector generating the images. There is none. My eyes burn more from the thickening air.

So hard do I squeeze the dagger handle that I feel the carvings etching impressions into my fingers.

With trepidation, I approach a small rectangular mirror: A young, laughing girl surfaces, galloping on a chestnut Arabian. A distinguished figure with a single silver lock falling across his brow, on a gray stallion, playfully chases her across the desert dunes. A wailing birth sound echoes throughout the sand hills.

Unable to move, I am jarred to attention by a shadow slipping between two nearby jagged pieces. As I leaped towards the motion, hundreds of broken mirrors began to spin and weave silently, as if held by unseen dancers. The whirling reflections are blinding.

Groping through flickering light beams, I find myself facing a 12-foot jagged mirror. All the mirrors halt, as another scene unfolds: A teenage mother rocks a wailing bundle. When I press my nose against the glass, the screaming child does not have a face. From the corner of the mirror, a machine with a heartbeat slithers its tentacles around the mother and the swaddled crying bundle.

Easing my grip on the dagger I turn away reaching for the warmth of my amulet.

Forcing myself to look again reveals a young woman in an Academy uniform bullied by an aging commander with his medals dripping blood. She defiantly bares her breast before raising a fighting stick. Her blue Lotus tattoo brings a hush.

Running madly, *why am I reliving my past?*

A smoky, broken mirror about my height rushes forward and I collide with it. The mirror explodes into twin holograms.

My two archetypes Queen and Warrior stand shoulder to shoulder. The Queen speaks, "You are not a sparrow tossed about by the wind. You are a leader among women blessed with vulnerability and wisdom. You are empowered by a higher Spirit."

As the image of the Queen fades, Warrior whispers, "A sparrow can be whom she wants to be, even a falcon. Focus. Listen to the great Spirit speaking in your heart."

Looking around sniffling, *I am falcon. Concentrate on my prey.*

In this house of images, *Baba is the sparrow.*

As if my thoughts push a lever, all the mirrors begin to dance again. Covering my eyes from the painful erratic reflections, I question why my Lover archetype does not honor me with her presence.

Stumbling into an octagon mirror: A bright image of Father rises, bare chested, sweating and pruning the young myrrh bushes oozing golden sap. His tantalizing movements mesmerize the young girl watching. I feel the glow in her cheeks and breasts. The young commander jumps from his Jeep, raises a whip, and wrestles Abba to the ground.

On second thought, *didn't I close my heart to Abba? Creating a vacancy I attempted to fill with my assassin's job. Then Samman and Zagh are surrogates, not real lovers.*

An apparition materializes to my left. But the jagged mirrors initiate a new rhythmic performance, flickering beams of light. The shadow disappears.

With my hands outstretched I grope in the figure's direction. I collide with a rectangular mirror and face a noisy bazaar, a ballet of weathered faces, belching motorcars, and clanking trishaws.

I hear the lyrical sounds of Mandalay.

More images form. A hulk in an exquisite white suit, dances with a dark-haired comedian. They laugh and sing, "Little Sparrow one, Little Sparrow three. Catch us if you can." The white form carrying a wailing lump in his arms runs in one direction while the black figure skips in another, tearing up pages of poetry.

There is no escape.

In anger, I raise my dagger and strike at the mirror, shattering the images. Cornered I want to flee the past. The shards of glass crunch under my boots as I begin to sprint.

My elbow hits a colossal mirror, which begins a slow spin pushing me into another jagged mirror. Crushing more glass, I ricochet into yet another irregular mirror, and then another, and another. Soon most of the jagged glasses are twirling and wobbling like an army of children's tops.

Disoriented I close my eyes, *cannot fight the unknown.*

Once more I thrust out my dagger and the army of jagged mirrors stands at attention. Touching the closest oblong piece: an image of a silver hot air balloon rises against a backdrop of a thousand points of golden pagodas. In the balloon basket, a woman with lavender cropped hair laughs at her lover with raven hair. A swallowtail butterfly with blue wings flutters towards them. Reaching for the butterfly the woman tumbles from the basket. Transformed into a butterfly she struggles to fly into his arms.

"Petition God to bless me immortal to search forever for love," cries the butterfly.

The raven hair shouts, "Your God abandoned you." With his fists, he beats the butterfly which tumbles downward.

Bolting, I crash into another glass reflection, scattering fragments of mirrors like fireflies. Spinning to avoid the glass insects, I confront a narrow slice of mirror: I watch myself as a Princess listening to a Magi bartering, "more gold. Wine for the poor, and strong camels, are pricey." The figure changes into Commandant Sam.

"My ramshackle world is crumbling," I shout above the grinding shards beneath my boots. Something warm is running down my hand. From the flying glass, a thin stream of my blood appears on the dagger handle.

To the far right, the dark shadow slides between two reflections.

Searching for an opening between two mirrors, I am confronted by a four-foot rolling glass. It displays: a red balloon child chased by two tortoiseshell cats. A faceless rider on a stallion appears, snatching the boy balloon which ruptures it. My heart makes no sound at the balloon's bursting cries.

In my rush to break free from this nightmare, I knock into a wobbling trapezoid mirror: A small dagger surfaces, flashing a silver blade, its handle from twisted tree roots drips blood. The dagger jitterbugs with an ancient Glock, with a smiling liberty lady handle. A noxious shadow splits them apart. The dagger assails the shadow but instead stabs the smiling lady liberty. The images dissolve into lightness. Moving closer to the mirror surface, I see a sparrow on its back, fluttering.

A shaft of outside brightness pains my eyes. I squint to watch the shadow escape through the open door. I race towards the light, dragging the shards which cry and groan like the damned.

At the exit falling to my knees sobbing, *when my employer discovers my failure, yet again, they'll stake my naked body on a real desert to wait for night vermin to gather for a feast.*

Fifty-Four

My sparrow mind stretches, cracking. My skull throbs. Swaying on the circus top I'm not sure anymore if what I recall is true.

 Drip.
Drop plop.
Splash spatter splat.
I visualize water lilies blooming
in the desert, the Black Blizzard soaking
into the sands.

The rains come pounding the Cirque du Grati complex.

Outside the house of images, I lift my face to heaven. Opening my blouse, the torrent washes my tattoo. *Raining goats and cats—but will it cleanse me of all my mistakes?*

Nearby, in a dilapidated circus tent, I seek refuge. Warily I creep past the shadows. My drenched suit dumps dark pools on the sawdust. My tangled hair is not a lavender halo above blacken eyes.

Among the menagerie of tigers and panthers, a stooped figure scoops dung near the gate of a cage. *Could he finally be Baba?*

The cage, no ordinary den for beasts, is rectangular, but seemingly without corners, a small island. The immense edifice floats a foot above nothingness. From beneath the structure belches smoke of the foulest of smells.

Bars, like thick warriors, march around the perimeter. *Incarcerating my victim or preventing intruders?* "Never could imagine such an underworld," I whisper, not wanting to alert the stranger.

The downpour gnaws on the overhead canvasses causing greater rips. *It's much too easy. Hunter and prey brought together in this hellish scene.*

Above the gate, an iron scroll proclaims in ancient hieroglyphics, *Those who enter*, and the words are immediately interpreted in my mind, *at your own risk,* I wince, continuing to decipher, *All are lost who enter.*

Gingerly I push the massive gate inward with little effort. Then like a falcon I swoop into the den and confront the hunched figure.

"Prince Baba shovels shit well." The urge is to laugh, but I can't, since he performs his labor seriously. "Of all the places on earth or in Hades to finally catch you, my elusive quarry."

The bent figure straightens slightly on his shovel and turns to face me, "Whom did you say I am?"

"I see your scar and that ridiculous goatee."

"Disguises are easily come by."

"Baba is a slippery monster. A devil," I emphasize to fuel my anger to eradicate him.

"In addition to name calling, do you concede I am perhaps your father?" And thinks, *I'm weary of this game.*

"In your eyes the fire does not burn as bright. And you smell of animal dung, not the earthy odor of frankincense. Besides my Abba, is dead. You, Baba, stand before me, flesh and blood!" I wonder, *truly don't comprehend this man even after chasing his shadow across half the globe.*

"Princess, who do you believe I am?" A hint of nobility returns to his eyes.

"I'm not your Princess," I shout and the wild beasts murmur, swaying back and forth. "Yet I have the power to exterminate or save you."

"You will always be my little Princess. Remember where your power originates." He points upward and my eyes follow.

"God abandoned me. And Baba did not have a daughter, only a son. In this moment and place," raising my voice, "be aware of my authority. I am your executioner and confessor." Pacing rapidly, the wild cats are now moaning and groaning, showing their disapproval of my tone.

He responds in silence and considers, *How can I convince her of whom I am and my innocence?*

"I'm exhausted from hunting you. Don't know what evils you perpetrated on the Coterie's organization, but your sins must be great if they want you eliminated."

"My mistake is no greater than striving to continue breathing. Samman through his agent Jeune coerced me to take on Baba's appearance by cutting a scar and growing a goatee. This was rather easy because Baba and I could be doubles."

"Sam forced you? I don't believe it."

"Jeune thinks Samman is making a power play for his father's position as Supreme Commander. Simply he wants Baba dead.

"Now you imply Sam would have his own father murdered to gain control." I shake my head speculating, *could I have my own Abba killed for any reason?*

"An individual can become a shadow of whom we expect. In the case of your Sam, he deceived both of us. He gave me the hope of living longer to complete the formula. And to my innocent daughter—perhaps the prospect of love."

"Don't drag my relationship with Sam into your trial to cloud my judgment." I stomp my foot and the animals snarl.

"Did he torture you?"

"No. He provided a valise of Credits to fund my research and finance my escape."

"Aha, I knew it came down to wealth," shaking my head.

"No, not at all, the Farafra farm was failing and I couldn't afford to continue the hybrid research. Impersonating Baba seemed a small price.

"What did Baba do to deserve the death sentence?"

"You mean other than have a son like Sam?" He attempts a grin, "I believe Baba is living too long and Sam wants the leadership now. Through the InterSocial false deeds were spread incriminating Baba."

"Thought the InterSocial was created only to promote good and fuzzy news," raising my eyebrows.

"Yeah, I agree, but Sam was somehow able to manipulate narratives. Nice upstanding enterprise you work for."

"You're employed by the same wonderful syndicate. If you aren't Baba I imagine they had you cut him up into bite-size pieces for the desert beasts."

"The real Baba, according to Jeune, was convinced by Sam to visit the Americas. Not surprisingly he stayed because he purchased a franchise called Love & Liberty Cream Ice stores. Perhaps you've seen them? Anyway, Sam still needs to present a corpse to the Corterie which is where I come in."

"You're telling tall tales like I heard when I was a child. Why would Baba relinquish ruling the most powerful organization in the world in order to scoop frozen treats? Humor me. Why should I believe you?"

"Perhaps Baba just had enough and fancied he could stay alive by retiring. On the other hand, I wanted nothing to do with the Coterie. Your Sam demanded the formula.

For good or evil reasons I'm not sure. Threatened to kill me. Cut off my head if I did not finish the formulation while hiding as Baba in the monastery." His shoulders droop, "I had no idea this cunning Coterie would hire my daughter to assassinate Baba." Grinning, ". . . a rather inept assassin at that."

"You're criticizing my skills when you can't finish a simple formula," I yell. "Like an idiot, I pursued someone in the guise of Baba across Tibet, among the Bristlecone pines and through this circus," sidestepping to avoid a gush from the thinly stretched circus top. "My Ballyhoo uncle, who brought all the dirty assignments didn't trust me with the amazing fact that you are alive?"

"My brother did not share his moonlighting or my new identity with you because Samman threatened both of us. The game of pursuit had to appear real to you." His demeanor changes to that of a youthful schoolboy telling of a great adventure. "The crowning achievement was to fake my death in order to extract me from my old life and to buy time to finalize the formula before you located me." His eyes kindle some of the old fire. "Without a home or country, I played a most dangerous game."

"Think that Farafra oasis nurtured a fool? It sounds as if Jeune and you are play-acting with me. My head hurts."

"Sam hoped you could convince me to come back and reveal the final formula. Later Jeune explained that if you killed me the Coterie won either way with or without the formulary. Simply put, they wanted to destroy it, but were curious about the particulars. Economically, the misfortunes of the pandemic fill their pockets. And remember, Sam requires a cadaver."

"Your story is unbelievable. Why keep running?"

With tearful eyes, he says, "In the monastery and the Bristlecones Theatre when you were ever so close I wanted to reveal myself. But they would have hired another assassin for both of us."

"Return with me and we'll straighten out this mess."

"If I go back they will torture and most likely kill me. The details of the formula are only in my memory."

"You best start writing very precise notes."

Distorting his face with a long pause he reveals, "the antidote is fictitious. At this time there is no reliable cure for the Black Blizzard diseases. After all these years my research has failed. Even the exotic perfume is a fiasco. The Coterie will never believe my story."

"I don't accept it either. Your excuses become more incredible and are distracting from my mission to eradicate you."

In desperation, he squints at the bulging circus tent top and the leaking seams. "It's more likely this deluge will wash away the Black Blizzard than a reliable remedy is developed."

"My world is eroded from under my feet." I shake my drenched hair on a nearby panther who licks the moisture from its paws. After a long hesitation, I throw my hands in the air proclaiming, "Now I understand. There aren't two individuals. Baba and Abba don't just look alike; they are one and the same."

"What? Have you lost your senses?" He laughs then abruptly stops.

"That's why you were away from Farafra so often. You were leading a double life as Supreme Commander of the Coterie and research guru with us. Samman isn't your son; he's your henchman. The Coterie wised up to your shenanigans and, shall we say politely, is removing you from office by assassination."

Father chuckles, then turns serious, "Never was or pretended to be two different personalities or lead two lives. And I definitely am not the real Baba who is living splendidly in the Americas. Daughter, look deep into my eyes."

A million universes and far-flung stars explode in his gaze. Blinking again and again, *No, what I really observe is a tired Abba worried about whether his frankincense and myrrh hybrids are surviving.*

"Well, what do you see?"

"My eyes are blinded by your lies."

"My precious Lilee, take the rocks out of your eyes so you can see the pebbles in mine."

"What do you mean? You're treating me like a little child."

"Remove those huge obstacles like fear and anger from your sight so that you can observe my small faults." He motions towards his chest, "Look once more with your heart."

After several moments, "I see a compassionate spirit," but think, *can't accept you're Father if I'm to kill* . . . Then add quickly, "you could be Abba."

"Ah, we are making progress. Just to be clear. Samman and Zagh do not work for me. And Zagh is Sam's Lieutenant."

"Zagh can't be," I scream. "I sensed his love was weak, but given another chance possibly his heart could be transformed."

"As a loyal Flag he took an oath to abstain from earthly love, nonetheless he surely has deep affection for the Coterie."

"Enough lies about Zagh." Lashing out, "I pray your deceiving brother drives off a desert cliff. Don't trust him as far as I can heave his charming British Hulk."

"Incidentally Jeune informs me that your Sam and Zagh manipulated you and even seized your child." He speculates, *am too spineless to reveal that your son is not real.* Then adds, "In fact, your two so-called lovers could be watching right now to make certain you complete your task."

"You're fabricating stories again."

"No, no look around," he emphasizes and thinks, *I need time to work up courage to convince Lilee that her child is an imagination created by an evil machine.*

"Hey affectionate Sam and beloved Zagh, show your cowardly faces. Do your own dirty work," I shout to the darkness beyond the cage.

A brief echo is the only response.

"Humpty Dumpty Uncle is never around when I need him. Most likely cavorting with sweet Madame." Pummeling these words at Father, I catch a flash of a white suit near the tent entrance.

"Your uncle is loyal and most likely nearby observing. You know he really loves you, like I do."

"Uncle has a strange way of showing his affection like you do. Except both of you seem to desire Madame."

"Difficult woman to love, your mother."

"She never appreciated anything I did," I growl.

"Madame loves the exhilaration of the circus. Once observed her shape shift into an albino serpent. Wouldn't doubt that she worked hand-in-hand with the Coterie to remove you from me. Her mischiefs are almost as disastrous as my brother having to fake marrying her to facilitate my covert actions."

Twisting away, "The picture you paint sickens me: walking hand-in-hand with a transmuting white snake woman, my Humpty Dumpty uncle and my withered branch of a father, if indeed you are my biological father. I'm beginning to doubt it the way you act. You are a teller of tall desert tales." The animals mirror my passion by pacing, ready to strike to protect their cage keeper.

"Perchance Madame slithered away and joined another circus." His attempt at humor falls flat. "Look at me." I turn once again to face him. "For all that I have done to deceive you, I am truly sorry. Can you not find it in your heart to forgive your Abba?"

"You've tricked me too many times. Your ultimate betrayal was to hire Sam to seduce your own daughter for some hideous reason—perhaps to save your darling hybrids."

The beasts circle closer and closer snarling at me.

"Never Princess, never. Unexpectedly Samman arrived to check out the rumors about the formula. He pretended to fall in love with you to discover how much you knew."

"Desert rubbish," my mind swirls. "You best pray for forgiveness."

He places his hand on the closest scowling tigress and she curls into a fetal dream. In a gesture of what appears to be a blessing, he raises his hands over the grumbling menagerie. Their wild arguments reduce to a chorus of purring.

Over animals he has power. He can't be my father. Maybe a spirit. "Enlighten the universe and me how many innocents have you sentenced to death?"

Father throws up his arms. "My sweet Princess you are confusing Baba and me. InterSocial reports delighted in narrating Baba's mischiefs which Sam created and exploited to discredit him. I did not condemn a single soul, even a Flag. Am innocent."

"There is no one here—Jeune, Samman, Zagh—to substantiate your story. Justice must be served." Then think, *never have I been this close to executing anyone. My hands are shaking.*

"Compassion, Princess. You see it in my spirit. At Farafra didn't I teach you clemency towards all the creatures in the desert, even vile ones?

"My father never taught mercy towards my enemies. Instead he instructed me how to shoot."

"I cherish you more than my life."

"Abba cared for me, but he is dead. You are my foe and the adversary of my Coterie family."

He stands mute and bowed as a myrrh tree broken by the desert wind.

"It truly doesn't matter who you really are. You understand my task is to bring you back alive, but if you will not cooperate I must kill you. " My voice lacks the conviction of my verdict. Looking up at the bulging canvasses, "Wouldn't it be hilarious if this downpour did wash away the pandemic? It would almost solve our dilemma. But in the end you will be tortured to death because the Coterie will not believe your botched research story either."

"I can't surrender to the Coterie. Yet you have other options. Your decision to execute me will not save the world or the Coterie from their mistakes."

"It rescues my son. And I may not be able to conceive anymore."

"Aha yes, you trust the Coterie has your son and will release him if you deliver me." Perspiring, he doesn't have the courage to reveal the facts from Jeune that she delivered a fictitious son fabricated by a callous machine.

"Are you sweating because you know you're about to die?" Shaking my head, "Instinctively a mother knows that her son is still alive. Just as I understand you will never go back."

"Lilee, the assassin in you is irresponsible. My little Sparrow was not raised foolishly."

"I am no longer Lilee or a sparrow. My last trill will be the clattering tune of your death. The little sparrow has become a fierce falcon. My claws will tear out your heart to deliver it to my Coterie family." And thinks, *Where are my archetypal energies to strengthen me, to transform words into deeds?*

"Even a falcon shows mercy on its own kind. My Sparrow, the reason you are capable of flying to greater heights is my love and our family."

"I lost my wings and have no clan but the Coterie's. It would have been better that you were never born."

"Who would have helped to conceive you?" He attempts a laugh and mulls over, *dare I reveal that Sam is not the father of her imaginary son to persuade her from this course of death?*

"I would choose a better sire for myself. Just as I would have selected a better father than Sam for my son," I mumble gazing at my feet swelling in my soaked boots.

"You can't be that heartless, Princess. If you exterminate me what will happen to our history together?"

"Everything you imparted is now worthless. Your memories will be thrown into the same abyss I fell when I thought you were dead. I kept the blood map close to my heart as a remembrance of you. But all the blouses which touched your map will be burned." Throwing the map at his feet, I reflect, *won't give him the satisfaction before he dies that the real treasure is hidden in the Magi's dagger handle.*

"So be it if my body must descend into the depths of hell to show my love." He picks up the map and stuffs it in his shirt pocket.

"You don't love me. You love your hybrid plants."

"Remember our times together: listening to Scripture stories while sitting at my feet, riding the Arabians in the cool of the evening, even learning to shoot."

"I did believe in the Scripture parables which you explained especially *love one another . . . Better to give one's life* . . . but then you sold MY favorite Arabian, Roman and played a part in stealing my son."

"The family business was desperately poor. What I taught you is true." Again he throws up his arms. "If I must give my life for you and your son . . ."

"Don't pretend your frustrations. You are desperate. I will kill you and live happily forever with my son."

"I am an old, brittle branch. If you bend me, I'll . . ."

"There are forces beyond my assassin's control."

"Our lives are intertwined and fragile."

"I'm out of time. Your people will find us."

"I have no guards."

"Oh? Where are the legions to protect you? Those led by your Humpty Dumpty Ballyhoo brother?" Expecting to see the white suit pop-up I look around.

"None, only myself. Your Abba."

"Look at yourself, a dying man; your successes are shadows."

"If you execute your Abba, you will become a lonely sparrow lamenting her loss." His hands fall limp at his sides.

"No black armband will be worn on my falcon wing mourning your demise." I touch my left arm with the dagger taken from my back sash.

"If Lilee accomplishes this deed she will find no home in the temples of man or rest in the house of God."

"I can't forfeit my firstborn for your transgressions."

The accused stands mute, matched by the hush of the jury—the tigers and panthers.

"Lay your heart on this altar," I hold out my left hand. "The few remnants of my love for you require I sacrifice your soul for my son," I tighten my grasp on the dagger in my right hand.

"Does not your past love demand a little mercy?" Again he does not disclose the truth about the vile apparatus which created her child.

"First, ask for forgiveness," I stomp my soaked boot.

"If I must."

"From the Coterie's court," I grind my boot into the sawdust.

"No, only from you, my loving daughter."

"Forgiveness is bought with your sacrifice on this altar," stretching out my left hand further. "My son is not here to even consider as an alternative victim on this altar to appease my Coterie family." Squeezing the dagger harder, "Absolution carries a high price."

"They sold you a vision of motherhood and a relationship with a son that only exists in your memories. You last saw your son at birth. The snares of this world or the pandemic may already have sealed his fate."

"Do not insult my living son, your blood heir, your grandson."

"Be realistic." He shakes his head.

"As I said before a mother knows. I can feel my offspring's heartbeat." I pound the handle of the dagger against my heart.

"Would you sacrifice something real, standing here who loves you, for an unreal possibility, a dream?" For the third time, Abba resists revealing that a son lives only in her mind.

Now I stand silent. *My heart whispers that I still love Abba, with all his faults.*

"What does your spirit say?" Father speaks softly.

Absorbed by his voice I respond, ". . . forfeited my soul."

"Come again? What do you mean—relinquished yourself?" He moves a little closer.

"Abandoned my soul to my new Coterie family with each bungled killing assignment." I smile weakly and suppose, *the courageous warrior falcon is reduced to a little sparrow. If only I could fly to a sanctuary and play my life over again without the same mistakes.*

"Don't let your bad acting as an assassin deceive you." Abba holds out his hands. "More significantly you love your son unconditionally without actually knowing him. But killing me will not bring him back. If they have your son he will never be released. Forever he will be dangled above your head to do their dirty work."

"For a lousy profession and to belong to a dysfunctional family, I've hawked my soul."

"Precious Lilee, you are too callous. In simple terms, will my daughter continue to tolerate the Coterie's power over her life?"

"With promises I dearly wanted to hear, my Coterie family bought me for their killing arm. After losing your love I gave myself freely to them and Zagh and others without anything in return. *Perhaps there is a way I can regain your love.*

"Princess, I didn't always show my feelings. It's difficult for me to even hug you. Trust me, I love you.

He moves nearer to embrace me.

A powerful fire overwhelms my entire being.

"Love wins in the end." Breathing slowly, "I can give life, even if it's not another child."

My left hand touches him gently on the cheek like a kiss.

Ripping the amulet from my neck, I plunge the dagger deep into my heart, collapsing into Abba's arms.

The bellow of the beasts rises in crescendo, a melody of love.

**From the murky waters
rises Lilee,
the exquisite blue
lotus unfurls white
And angels join the chorus.**

Fifty-Five

A tiny ember in my sparrow heart flares. At long last my spirit listens to my heart

 Vast sheets of the pavilions collapse from the monsoons. Thousands of incandescent lights pop in unison. Countless short-circuiting electronics flash and die. Doused technicians scurry in panic. The great Cirque is torn apart.

In contrast, drenched audiences, performers, and beasts are brought to a standstill. A wonder-filled stillness girds the darkness.

After wiping his eyes, Abba carries and rests me, his Lilee, his Lotus, on the gate threshold. From his pocket he returns the gold ring to my little finger.

Rising he looks about, listening.

In the Cirque, life reawakens with a determined heart-beat.

When Abba turns to where he laid me, I am gone. Only my amulet remains at the entrance. Gazing skyward, "My little She Sparrow soars once more."

THE END

.

Surrounded by his Japanese gardens, Ted Zahrfeld resides in Michigan with his cat, Torti.

His first novel, *she sparrow*, was born out of a near-death experience while sailing.

Currently he is crafting the novel, *Tenir*, the escapades of an American journalist who would forsake love to thwart "the war to end all wars."

His collection of poems, *Christmas Days & Beyond*, will be published in 2018.